NICHOLAI GALOV
IS TWO MEN.

ONE IS CALLED HERO.

THE OTHER . . .

George Markstein's newest thriller,
a novel of KGB betrayal, CIA treach-
ery, and a spy on the run from them
both!

Also by George Markstein
Published by Ballantine Books:

THE GOERING TESTAMENT

CHANCE AWAKENING

TRAITOR

GEORGE MARKSTEIN

BALLANTINE BOOKS • NEW YORK

There is no Soviet Consulate in Frankfurt, but the anatomy of the defection is based on fact.

Copyright © 1981 by George Markstein

Originally published in England in October 1979 by The Bodley Head, under the title of TRAITOR FOR A CAUSE.

All rights reserved under International and Pan-American Copyright Conventions. Published in the United States by Ballantine Books, a division of Random House, Inc., New York.

Library of Congress Catalog Card Number: 80-68852

ISBN 0-345-28609-X

Manufactured in the United States of America

First Edition: February 1981

Manhattan

The doorbell sounded its warning as the man in the steel-framed glasses came into the stampshop from the street.

Peter Klass, philatelist, whose shop front proclaimed CASH FOR STAMPS, RARE ISSUES BOUGHT AND SOLD, looked up at the stranger. He was holding a stamp with a pair of tweezers, about to slide it into the pocket of an album.

"Dobriy dyehn," said the man pleasantly. He had blue eyes and wore a belted raincoat.

Klass put down the tweezers. Beneath his bushy gray eyebrows, he looked suddenly suspicious. "I do not speak Russian," he said, but his accent betrayed the lie.

"Oh, I'm sorry," said the man. "I said good afternoon." His smile was disarming as he stood in front of the counter, gazing around at the colorful array of stamps exhibited under glass. "You have some interesting items," he added.

Klass shut the album in front of him.

"What is it you are looking for?" he asked. His tone was unfriendly.

"I am sure you have it," smiled the stranger. "Cosmonauts."

"I don't understand." Klass sounded as unhelpful as he meant to be.

"I would like to see some stamps about space exploration," said the stranger. "Moon shots. Space missions. Astronauts. You know the kind of thing."

"You mean, commemoratives. . . ." Klass sniffed. "They are not very valuable. Schoolboy stuff."

The man in the steel-framed glasses wasn't discouraged. "One day they will be valuable," he said easily. "And anyway, I like the pretty pictures."

Klass hesitated. Then he suddenly asked, like a man who had decided to take the plunge. "You are Russian?"

"I'm a stamp collector. In an amateur sort of way, you understand."

Klass got off his stool behind the counter. "I think you've come to the wrong shop," he said. "This is really for specialists."

The man looked around again. "Oh, I'm sure you can help me," he insisted. "Quite certain, in fact."

Outside, a police-car siren sounded. The stranger, that gentle smile on his face, did not take his eyes off Klass.

"Don't worry, I can always come back," he suggested mildly. "If it is not convenient now."

"No, no." Klass shook his head vehemently. "That will not be necessary. Perhaps I have what you want. Very cheap, but it may be what you're looking for."

He bent under the counter and produced a small green album. "Here." He opened the stiff pages, and from neat rows of new, fresh-looking stamps took one out with his tweezers.

"This commemorates the Viking missions to Mars," explained Klass. "Unmanned space flights in '75 and '76. The fifteen-cent issue." He held out the tweezer hopefully.

"I'd rather see a Soviet space stamp," said the stranger. "Please take your time."

"Well . . ." Klass put the stamp back. "I happen to have these." He extricated another scrap of paper from the back of the album. "The Soyuz space rocket. It is a whole set. Fifteen kopeks is the Sirena experiment, and thirty-two kopeks the space station Komarov."

The stranger beamed. "That's more like it," he said. "I think I'd like those."

"Very well," muttered Klass. He started to put the stamps into a transparent envelope.

"Do you mind if I have a cigarette?" asked the man politely.

Klass shook his head.

The man produced a pack, offered it to Klass. "Would you like one?"

Klass shook his head.

The man put the cigarette in his mouth and pulled out a gold cigarette lighter. He was standing in front of Klass and quite close to him. He flicked the lighter.

An almost invisible jet of vapor shot straight out of the lighter into the stamp dealer's face. For a moment, Klass stared in surprise at his customer. Then, suddenly, a spasm of agony twisted his face. He dropped the little envelope with the stamps and clutched his chest. He staggered and fell across the counter.

The man with the steel-rimmed glasses put the lighter back in his pocket. The unlit cigarette was still in his mouth. Almost delicately, he gave the body of Klass a

2

gentle little push, and it slid to the floor, hidden from view behind the counter.

The man walked out of the shop, turned right along West Forty-fifth Street, and was lost in the crowds before he had reached Fifth Avenue.

Frankfurt

"You are not here, are you?" said Shura. It was more an accusation than a question.

"What do you mean?" asked Nicolai.

"Here, with me, in this apartment. You're somewhere else, miles away. You lay beside me like a plank of wood in the bed. All night. You've hardly noticed me this morning." Her voice softened. "What is the matter, Nicolai?"

She still looked very attractive, he decided. The dark housecoat showed off her fair color, and though it hid the contours, he needed no reminding of her body underneath.

"I'm sorry," said Nicolai. "I've got a lot on my mind."

"If there is a problem, you must share it." Her green eyes pleaded with him.

"I always do," he lied. He went out onto the balcony of their small flat in the Wieserstrasse, ten minutes from the consulate, and felt the soil of the plants they were growing there.

"I watered them yesterday," said Shura.

"You're very methodical always," Nicolai nodded approvingly. "It's a great virtue." He looked at his watch. "I shall be late."

She leaned over the breakfast table, picked a cigarette out of the wooden box, took the lighter out of her housecoat pocket, and lit it. Then, blowing out a cloud of smoke, she asked, almost casually: "The new man is due today, is he not?"

"Rostov? Yes."

"Are you meeting him at the airport?"

"He's already here. He arrived from Berlin yesterday."

"Oh." She looked surprised. "Is he in your department?"

"He will be ranked as a vice consul, that's all I know." His tone was final.

But Shura kept at it. "Is his family with him?"

Nicolai hesitated. "I don't know," he said at last.

It annoyed him, the way she had recently been getting more curious about the consulate, the people there, his own activities. She, the daughter of a Red Army colonel, a child of the state, should know better.

"I look forward to meeting him," pressed Shura.

He allowed himself a wry smile. "I'm sure you will, babushka."

He gave her a perfunctory kiss on the cheek, and then she stood on the balcony and watched him get into the little Volkswagen with the special diplomatic plate and drive off.

Nicolai Galov, vice consul, member of Section II of the KGB's 1st Chief Directorate, would soon be at his desk at the Consulate-General of the U.S.S.R. in Frankfurt.

Shura saw the black Mercedes pull out of its place by the curb and slowly start to follow Nicolai's Volkswagen.

She smiled.

Manhattan

In death, Klass's waxen face almost expressed relief. As the container with his body slid out of the refrigerated cabinet, the white-coated attendant checked the tag attached to his foot.

"That's him," he said.

Bishop stared down at the corpse. He had not seen Klass for a long time.

"Fingerprints and dental work check," confirmed O'Shea. He was from homicide, and he didn't like being kept in the dark. First the peculiar interest shown by a taciturn man from the FBI who wouldn't explain why it concerned him, and now the appearance of Bishop. None of it jelled.

"Anything else you want?" asked O'Shea.

"Not right now."

Bishop gave Klass one last look as the body rolled back into its iced darkness.

"This way," said O'Shea. Their footsteps echoed in the morgue corridor.

In the car, O'Shea asked: "You from Washington?"

"Yes," said Bishop curtly.

O'Shea wanted to ask more. A lot more. All the man from the FBI had told him was that somebody called Bishop would be in touch, and please cooperate fully.

Here he was, the tall man with the gray hair, in his gray suit. A plain blue shirt, a nondescript tie with some kind of club motif. In appearance, almost monastic, as befitted his name. A bishop in Brooks Brothers vestments.

"What's your interest in this?" asked O'Shea.

"You read the medical examiner's report?"

"Sure," said O'Shea. "That's why I'm on the case. It wasn't the heart attack we thought. It's not kosher, but that doesn't make it a federal matter, does it?"

"Traces of prussic acid in his stomach, tiny flakes of glass on his face. No, not kosher," agreed Bishop. But he didn't answer the question.

O'Shea looked straight at him. "You've got an idea, haven't you? You know what it's all about?"

Bishop stared out the car window, as if he hadn't heard.

"Who the hell was this guy anyway?" O'Shea pressed. "No family, no relations. We got nothing on him. Lived by himself. No friends. Who wants to waste him? What for?" He shook his head. "And what a crazy way to do it. What kind of weapon am I looking for?"

"I don't think you'll find it, but it'll be an interesting gadget," said Bishop suddenly communicative. "It's some kind of device with a spring that detonates a tiny glass ampule of prussic acid that's been loaded inside it. The poison is sprayed right into the victim's face."

O'Shea's mouth opened wide, but there was no sound.

"The effect is to cause instantaneous contraction of the victim's blood vessels, as in a sudden cardiac arrest. The victim dies on the spot, and it looks to all the world like a fatal heart attack." Bishop was like a lecturer before a class. "Sometimes nothing is detected, but luckily this city has a good medical examiner."

"I never heard of such a thing. . . ." gasped O'Shea.

"Neither had Scotland Yard when somebody jabbed the tip of an umbrella into a man in London, releasing a tiny metal ball into his thigh," Bishop sighed. "Smaller than a pinhead, that puncture mark, but he died, all right. They've still got no antidote to the poison in the little ball. Ricin, twice as deadly as a cobra's venom."

The car had stopped at the traffic light, and they both

sat, silently, abstractedly watching the throng of people crossing in front of them.

Bishop nodded at the passersby. "You see that man? With the can? Or the fat woman with the big purse? That guy carrying the package? Could be anybody like that. And it could be a fountain pen. A flashlight. Maybe even a watch, or a ring . . . anything. Anywhere."

The light changed to green and the car started to move again.

"The guy in London, who died—who was he?"

"A defector," said Bishop. "A defector who thought he was safe."

Frankfurt

From the outside, the consulate in the Beethovenstrasse looked like the residence of a wealthy, long-established bourgeois family. On the top floor, there were a couple of windows with bars, but that could be the nursery, made safe against an inquisitive toddler climbing out. There was a cluster of antennae on the roof, but only an expert would know they weren't just there to receive TV programs. And the single flagpole was usually bare, except for one or two occasions a year.

Nicolai parked his Volkswagen in one of the spaces reserved for consular staff. Two green-uniformed Schupos were at their post, the token presence, day and night, of West German authority. Their hair needed cutting, thought Nicolai. Or maybe long hair was a symbol of democracy.

If Nicolai was aware of the black Mercedes that had shadowed him, he gave no hint. Instead, he matter-of-factly pressed the top door button twice. The security man who opened the door nodded to him; so did his colleague, who sat at the table inside the reception hall, under the Foreign Ministry–issued framed picture of Lenin.

Recently, Nicolai had started looking at his surroundings with new eyes. Eyes like a camera, seeking to record the present for the future, like an archivist preparing to store memories in a file, knowing he would one day recall them lovingly.

He passed the waiting room, with its empty chairs lining the wall under Intourist and Aeroflot posters. The waiting room was usually empty, except when somebody came for a visa. That wasn't very often.

He took the lift to the basement and walked to the steel door. Behind it lay the restricted area, the Referentura. Behind that door, no outsider was allowed. Nor were most of the consular staff. The Referentura was the private world of the KGB.

Nicolai pushed the buzzer, and Leonid's eye peered out at him through the spy hole. Officially a clerk, Leonid was one of three armed men who divided the twenty-four hours of the day guarding the steel door. No passes, no ID cards, no code words effected entry: only the face.

The steel door slid aside, and Nicolai entered the antechamber.

"Nice day," said Leonid. It struck Nicolai as incongruous, the man with the shoulder holster, buried here behind steel and cement, where daylight never entered, commenting about the sunshine outside.

"Yes," said Nicolai.

Two more doors faced him, both double-locked. One was Communications, the center for ciphers, codes, radio transmissions. For the other door he had a key. But there were two locks: the KGB men who were privy to it carried one; the duty guard had the other key. No one could unlock the room by himself.

Nicolai pulled out his key, and Leonid inserted his own.

"Will you be long?" asked Leonid.

Nicolai shook his head. He crossed into the room, and its door was locked behind him.

Frankfurt did not have a particularly large Referentura. Compared to the ones in places like New York, Washington, San Francisco, London, Paris, and Rome, it was small. But like the others, it was equipped to block any kind of long-range electronic surveillance from the outside world. It had its own air conditioning and an emergency generator in case power in the rest of the building failed—or was cut off. Smoking down here was forbidden.

There was a table in the middle of the space with half a dozen chairs. Here the section could hold top-secret conferences and classified briefings that no one else in the consulate was entitled to know about.

Set in the wall was the safe. The safe that held the section's secrets. The safe to which only the representatives of Section II knew the current combination.

Representatives like Nicolai.

He stared at it for a long time, but he did not touch it. Leonid, watching the closed-circuit surveillance monitor in the antechamber, could scrutinize the screen all he liked.

Instead, Nicolai pulled out another key and unlocked the steel cabinet in the corner. He took out the black folder that contained the last twelve hours' messages and signals from headquarters. It was routine procedure, to keep yourself up to date about everything that had come in while you'd been off duty.

Keys turned in the door, and a stout, fresh-faced man came in. When he saw Nicolai, he smiled.

"So," said Rostov. "Reading the state secrets. That's very incriminating, this eagerness, before you've even put your feet up."

Nicolai put the file down and came forward.

"Welcome," he said.

They had met before, once in Pankow, once in London. Rostov was older than Nicolai, in his forties, and senior in rank.

"I was much happier coming to this post when I knew you were here." Rostov's eyes twinkled. "Tell me, how is your captivating Shura? As beautiful as ever?"

"You will see yourself, Ivan Ivanovitch."

"I hope so, I really hope so." Rostov looked pleased. Then, suddenly, he asked: "How are things here?"

Nicolai hesitated. "All right."

"Only all right? Not very good? Not excellent?"

"You will see for yourself," said Nicolai. He flicked through the file quickly. "There seems nothing new since last night." He started to put it back in the steel cabinet, but Rostov held out his hand.

"I think I will study it," he said. "I have much to learn about what is going on here."

Momentarily, their looks met. Then Nicolai shrugged. "Forgive me, then. I have things to do in my office."

He rapped on the steel door and started unlocking his side.

"Of course," said Rostov. "Please carry on. Perhaps we will have tea later."

After the door had been locked from the other side, Rostov put the file down. He went over to the safe and gently touched the combination lock, like a man exploring something.

Then he stared at the door through which Nicolai had departed, as if he wanted to pierce the steel and follow him.

His eyes were no longer twinkling.

Beverly Hills

Jimmy struck the wrong key, and Silkin wanted to hit him.

"Pay attention," he snarled. How he loathed the fat little boy, with his thick lips and freckled nose. How he wanted to grab the stupid, spoiled child and shake him until that empty head fell off.

Jimmy pouted. For his part, he had no great liking for Silkin, the gaunt, humorless man whom his mother had decided was to teach him the piano. Silkin was no fun at all, and when Mother asked how Jimmy was getting on, he made life difficult by saying things like "I'm afraid he's very lazy," or "He doesn't do his practice, you really must talk to him." And that meant more trouble.

Silkin came twice a week to give Jimmy lessons. Jimmy had contempt for this thin-faced man who spoke in a hard accent, because he knew Silkin detested the sessions as much as he did but presumably swallowed his dislike because he needed the money. Jimmy's parents were very rich, and Jimmy was very spoiled; he was disdainful of people who weren't just as rich. Jimmy was, in fact, quite unlovable.

"If you don't want to play the piano, say so," growled Silkin, "and stop wasting my time."

Scowling, Jimmy misplayed the scale again and Silkin winced.

"All right," he said curtly. He stood up. He was tall with a military bearing. "That is enough for today."

Jimmy slammed down the lid of the Bechstein. "Okay," he said sullenly.

Silkin picked up the silver-topped cane he invariably carried. It was the one thing about him that aroused a flicker of interest in Jimmy. He had once picked up the cane, just to look at it, and Silkin grabbed it from him.

"Don't touch my things," he had spat out, so fiercely that Jimmy's bulbous lips trembled and he had nearly cried. Nobody had ever talked to him that roughly. Since

9

then, the cane had fascinated Jimmy, but he had not dared to pick it up again.

After that episode, Jimmy had tried to get Silkin fired.

"Ma, I don't like him," he had protested. "Anyway, who wants to play that thing. Can't I have an electric guitar?"

Jimmy's mother wouldn't hear of it. The seven-year-old was the apple of her eye, and he could have everything in the world, as far as she was concerned. But she was determined that he learn the piano, and Silkin, peculiar accent and all, had a good reputation as a first-class teacher, expensive but brilliant.

"Never mind that you don't like him, just do as he says," she had replied. "I'm going to be so proud of you, you wait and see. Why, you'll play at Carnegie Hall one day, I bet."

Jimmy bit his lips. The injustice of it! It was so unfair.

"Ma . . ." he whined, but this was the one time he couldn't get his own way. So the lessons had continued, the cold war between Mr. Silkin and Jimmy getting chillier, and Jimmy's mother fondly imagining that a child prodigy was emerging.

"I'll be here Friday, as usual," announced Silkin. "And listen, young man, you'd better practice those scales for two hours a day. I warn you."

Jimmy still sat on the piano stool, but he swung his pudgy legs, as a sign of defiance.

"Do you understand?" asked Silkin.

Jimmy nodded.

"Well, say so."

"Okay," said Jimmy sullenly. "I'll practice."

The hell I will, he thought inwardly, and Mr. Silkin knew it.

"Otherwise I will have to talk to your mother again," he threatened, and stalked out of the huge room, with its glass wall looking out on the big lawn and the blue-tiled swimming pool.

As the piano teacher closed the door, Jimmy stuck out his tongue at him, with much feeling.

But Silkin never saw it. He crossed the hall just as Jimmy's mother appeared.

"Oh, I'm so glad I caught you," she cried. "How is it going? Is he making progress?"

"Well, madam," said Silkin in that formal, European way the Beverly Hills matrons adored, "it is hard work.

Jimmy is not, what is the word, pulling his weight. Perhaps you should tell him he must do better. He needs discipline."

"I'm sure you'll give him that. You are *so* good with him." She looked at her diamond-encrusted French wristwatch. "Oh dear, will you excuse me? I'm late for bridge, and the girls hate being kept waiting." She rushed out again.

Silkin said a very rude word in Russian under his breath, but the Filipino houseboy who opened the front door for him didn't even hear it, and if he had he wouldn't have understood its meaning.

Silkin emerged from the splendid house with its beautiful frontage and crossed the quiet street to his car.

He didn't even bother to look at the maroon Plymouth slowly coming toward him from the direction of Sunset Boulevard. It was really still too far away for him to take much notice.

.But suddenly the Plymouth accelerated, and Silkin looked up, startled, because it was hurtling at him with great speed. Such speed that he hastily jumped to one side.

But it was much too late, because the Plymouth was aimed at him, and the aim was true.

The car struck Silkin with such force that his body was flung into the air. It happened so quickly that he didn't even cry out, and he was dead before he hit the asphalt.

Jimmy, standing at a window, saw the Plymouth kill Silkin, mouth gaping. But as he rushed out of the room to tell everybody the news, he was grinning.

Not even Jimmy, though, got a good look at the driver, who was blue-eyed, wore steel-framed glasses, and never stopped.

Washington

The Admiral put down his cup of coffee and pushed it to one side. He had been having lunch in his office, and half the club sandwich was still on the small tray by the three telephones.

"Go on," he said quietly. He leaned back in his leather chair behind the big executive desk, flanked by the Stars and Stripes on his left, and the blue flag with the agency seal to his right.

"The L.A. police found the car, abandoned in Anaheim. Near Disneyland," said Bishop. On his lap rested the plain black binder containing the "Eyes Only" reports.

"Stolen?" asked the Admiral.

Bishop shook his head. "No, sir. It had been hired from the Hertz people at L.A. airport. The man produced a New York driver's license in the name of Lawrence Gottlieb."

"Credit card?"

"He paid cash for the deposit."

"Ah," said the Admiral. "Very suspicious, Carl. I thought nobody trusted people who pay cash."

"That's why the deposit. There *is* a Lawrence Gottlieb in Manhattan. He's been checked out. He lost his driver's license eight weeks ago. Or it was stolen."

"So?"

"That's all, sir," said Bishop. "Any useful fingerprints had been wiped away."

The Admiral's eyes had been called frosty when *Newsweek* ran a cover story on his appointment. Now, as they surveyed him, Bishop thought, once again, this guy is dangerous. He'll feed you to the sharks anytime.

"What exactly is your department's reading of the situation?" asked the Admiral.

That's right, said Bishop to himself. Suddenly it's my department, my baby, my responsibility.

But aloud he said: "It's pretty grim. Two defectors we've given sanctuary, new names, new backgrounds, new lives, are murdered. They found them, they killed them, and I don't think they're going to be the only ones."

The Admiral nodded.

"Bogdan Karlovski defected to us in Switzerland in '69, where he'd been a KGB illegal. You remember, he put the finger on that professor at Berkeley and the British Member of Parliament who was feeding them information."

"I remember," said the Admiral. "The British never did anything about it."

Bishop smiled austerely. "I guess it wasn't convenient for them. Anyway, Karlovski went undercover here, became Peter Klass. We set him up as a stamp dealer in New York. He's No. 1. Rudolf Gabrilovich came over in

12

'72, in Munich, their diplomatic cipher for Scandinavia in his pocket." He shook his head. "God knows why he wanted to teach the piano, but that was his business. He became Joe Silkin, and we got him a place in L.A. Now he's No. 2."

As he spoke, Bishop was trying to identify the squiggle the Admiral had begun drawing with a government-issue pencil on his notepad. It looked, from a distance, like a cobra coiling itself around.

"How long can we keep this under wraps?" asked the Admiral.

"Well, admiral," said Bishop, "we've been lucky so far. Nobody's realized who these two men really were. It's happened three thousand miles apart, and so far nobody's even linked the deaths. So far."

The Admiral got fed up suddenly with his little drawing, ripped the sheet off the pad, crumpled it up, and threw it into the wastebasket. Twice a day, a marine emptied the contents of that basket and burned them in an incinerator.

"You mean, it's only a matter of time?"

"Exactly," said Bishop.

"In a situation like this," and unexpectedly the Admiral had become expansive, "I always put myself in their mind. I try to forget who we are, and look at everything from their angle. You should try it, Carl."

Bishop remained silent.

"So I say to myself: What is the value of murdering two has-beens? I agree both these defectors had value when they came over to us and bought their passage with some useful material, but that was years ago. These men had become defunct, outdated, useless. We gave them fresh identities, anonymity. That was the reward for their treason."

Bishop's eyes flickered momentarily.

"But their importance, after all these years, is zero. My God, think how the world has changed since '69. So why bother about them now?"

"I think you know." Bishop's voice was very quiet.

"Oh, I see. You think, to discourage others. If they can show that we can't protect people, that the United States Government can't even safeguard the defectors it has given sanctuary, nobody will come over to us. It dries up the pipeline. Hmm. Maybe. Maybe you're right." He nodded to himself.

Bishop said the thing he had been waiting to say all the time. "I have a free hand, then, Admiral?"

The frosty eyes narrowed. "Free hand?"

"To find out what the hell's going on."

A fractional hesitation. Then: "Of course, Carl. And you've got me right behind you."

"Thank you, sir."

Bishop went to the door, but the Admiral called after him: "By the way, these defectors who are living under new colors, how many of them are there?"

Bishop turned. "Quite a few, Admiral."

"Living anonymously, with new identities, all over the place?"

"Yes, sir. All over the place."

"And who exactly knows where they are and who they are today?"

"Practically no one," said Bishop carefully.

"I want straight answers," barked the Admiral. "Exactly how many people?"

"Only two people can see that list," said Bishop.

"You'd better check into that," said the Admiral. "Do I know them? Who are they?"

"One is the President of the United States," said Bishop. "The other is me."

Frankfurt

Politeness was the keynote at the preview of the Pan African Art Exhibition in the Haus der Kultur. Nicolai presented his gilt-edged invitation card and joined the throng who, like him, were there to show the flag.

He smiled at the earnest girl from the British Council nodded courteously to the American vice consul, shook hands with somebody from the State of Hesse, exchanged a platitude with an official of the City of Frankfurt, and had a brief chat with the professor on the Slavonic faculty at the University. He ignored the U.S. two-star general and the exiled Bulgarian writer. Nicolai was there in his official capacity, as a representative of the Soviet Consulate, and he behaved officially.

A black man in white tribal dress, but with a smart dark suit visible underneath, made a short speech welcoming them "to this window on the Third World," and was suitably thanked by a junior minister who had come from Bonn. The black man was the diplomatic representative of an African state that had plenty of bauxite, cobalt, and manganese deposits, and the West German Government wasn't going to make a false step.

Nicolai and the others applauded with just the correct note of enthusiasm, and then the guests were free to roam around the exhibit. But Nicolai wasn't all that interested in the wooden carvings and roughly chiseled figures. He was looking for Haze.

He found him standing in front of a display of native masks from Ruanda.

"Mr. Haze?" he said.

Haze looked intense. He had a big forehead and a shock of brown hair, and when people got to know him they discovered he always looked intense, whether he was buying cheese, puffing his pipe, or interviewing Chancellor Schmidt.

"Yes?"

"I've wanted to meet you for a long time," said Nicolai. "I make a point of reading your column in the *Herald Tribune* every week. It's always very perceptive."

Haze, among other things, was one of the local contributors to the international paper.

"Thank you." He peered shortsightedly at Nicolai. "You are . . ."

"Nicolai Galov. I'm here with our consulate."

There was no need to say which consulate.

"Nice to meet you," said Haze. He nodded at the masks. "What do you think of them?"

Nicolai gave him a man-to-man smile. "A little primitive."

"Don't let them hear you say that. You have to call it a powerful example of ethnic art based on one of the world's oldest cultures."

"Is that how you're going to write about it?" asked Nicolai.

Haze shook his head. "I'm just freeloading. Where are the drinks?"

They found a waiter with a tray of champagne glasses.

"Must be a very interesting place, Africa," said Nicolai.

Haze shrugged. "I get mixed up with all the new names. Burundi, Lesotho, Botswana, Tanzania, Gabon—hell, there's dozens of them, and I don't know where one of them is."

"Your State Department does," said Nicolai.

Haze sipped his champagne. "Is this your line, Mr. Galov? Cultural activities?"

"I just shuffle papers. It can be very boring. Sometimes I wish . . ."

"Yes?" said Haze quietly.

"Well, take Africa. I'd love to see it."

"Really," remarked Haze, his eyes watching Nicolai very intently. "Maybe you'll get sent there one day."

"You're very lucky, Mr. Haze," said Nicolai, as if he hadn't heard him. "You go to so many interesting places. Journalists travel such a lot. They're not stuck behind a desk like me. . . ."

"You've got to be kidding. Look at me." Haze finished his champagne and beckoned to a waiter. "Just because I speak German, it's Bonn, Berlin, Frankfurt for me. Then, Frankfurt, Berlin, Bonn. If I'm lucky, it's Berlin, Bonn, Vienna. How does that grab you for wild excitement?"

"What about Munich?" asked Nicolai.

"Munich?" For an instant Haze's hand froze in midair around the new glass of champagne. Then he took a sip.

"Yes. You know, Radio Free Europe. You work for them too, don't you?" Nicolai looked very innocent.

"I'm a freelance," said Haze. "I work for a lot of people. Anybody who pays."

"Well," said Nicolai, and Radio Free Europe seemed forgotten, "one day maybe, I look forward to traveling to all these faraway places. All by myself. As free as a bird."

They were both silent. Then Haze asked, as if he were making small talk: "What kind of places?"

"Oh, I don't know. The places I read about. Mexico. Brazil."

"America?"

Their eyes met.

"Why not?" said Nicolai. "It sounds very interesting. I could find employment there. I imagine I could be an asset, don't you think?"

Haze put down his glass on a small table, beside a pile of exhibition catalogues.

"What about your wife?"

Nicolai looked surprised. "How do you know I'm married?" he asked.

"I guess I assumed it," said Haze. "You don't find many bachelor diplomats."

"My wife is no problem." Nicolai's tone was final.

"Well," said Haze, "this won't pay the rent. I'd better get going. This culture orgy isn't going to make five lines for me." He smiled at Nicolai. "Very pleasant meeting you." Haze gave him a final smile and walked off.

Nicolai showed close interest in the wooden carving of a witch doctor.

But inwardly he was thinking of other things.

On the whole, he reflected, it had all gone quite well. Or seemed to.

Munich

A car met him at the airport. It was Karstetter, driving himself.

"You picked a hell of a time," was his welcome. "Jeannie is about to produce the baby."

Haze wondered whether to say "I'm sorry," or "Congratulations."

"I can't take you back to the house," added Karstetter morosely. "She is so big she can't face people."

"Don't worry about it," said Haze.

"We'll go to the office," said Karstetter.

"Fine."

Karstetter, as always, looked the way he sounded, overburdened by his domestic responsibilities.

"Who's going to look after the children while your wife's in the hospital?" asked Haze, not that he could care less.

"Her mother," said Karstetter gloomily. "She's come over from Kansas City." He accelerated savagely. "Now what's all this about, Eddie?"

"I think we could be on to something big," said Haze. "Really big."

"Oh yeah?"

"I got a feeling one of their people in Frankfurt wants to defect."

Karstetter didn't even glance at him. He kept his eyes straight ahead.

"Who?" he asked.

"A man called Nicolai Galov. He's—"

Karstetter cut him short. "I know who Galov is," he said curtly.

"Well, I think he wants to come to us."

"Bullshit," said Karstetter.

"Listen, he as good as said so to me." Haze was annoyed. "I'm sure I'm right."

Karstetter sounded his horn savagely at an Audi with Augsburg plates that cut in front of him.

"You know what Galov really is?" he said. "He's a Section II man. Part of the 1st Directorate. He's one of the heavies. He's tied in with Department V. You know what that means? Wet affairs."

It was the trade euphemism for spilling blood. Karstetter's company preferred to call it executive action.

"Those guys don't defect," he added, like a mathematician proving an unchallengeable geometric theorem.

"I think this one is trying to." Haze could be very stubborn.

In the office, on the third floor of the anonymous building that most people thought housed a firm distributing American magazines in Europe, Karstetter listened to Haze's report.

Then he said: "Excuse me."

He picked up the phone, asked for an outside line, and dialed.

"How are you, honey?" he asked when a woman's voice answered. "Still nothing? Never mind, just relax. It'll come soon enough. Listen, I'm back at the office. Call me the moment—well, get your mother to call me. I'll be home soon anyway. See you."

He put the phone down, smiled apologetically at Haze.

"She's a little nervous. I know it's the third one, but you can't blame the poor kid. I'll be glad when it's over."

"What about Galov?" asked Haze.

"Ah yes, Galov." Karstetter's face clouded over. "I still think it's a load of bullshit. You got nothing to sell, Eddie. The guy comes up to you at some art show, says some vague thing about liking to travel, and you rush off all worked up. Forget it."

"Hold it." Haze was surprised at his own vehemence. "One, Soviet diplomats don't strike up casual conversations with strangers at functions. Two, it's not what he said, it's how he said it."

"Wrong again. You weren't a stranger to him. He knew your tie-up. Hell, he practically said so. That crack about Radio Free Europe . . ."

Haze shifted with frustration in his chair.

"Exactly. He wanted to make contact."

"You want coffee?" Haze shook his head. "There's nothing new about Soviet agents cultivating newspapermen. They're useful contacts. Maybe he was trying to recruit *you*, Eddie. You thought about that?"

"No," said Haze obstinately. "He was putting out feelers."

"Hell, he didn't even offer you bait. He didn't even hint he'd have some goodies for us."

"Jack, it's too early for that. Anyway, you said yourself Galov isn't exactly small fry. He's special."

Karstetter loosened his necktie. It was a thing he usually did within ten minutes of coming indoors.

"I say you're wrong. But, just supposing, what do you want me to do about it?"

Haze leaned forward eagerly. "Follow it up. Set up the machinery. Sure, let's be cautious, but let's find out. Sound him out. Establish a link. See how far he'll go."

Karstetter looked unhappy. "Bishop will never wear it," he said.

"Try him."

"And if it blows up in our faces?"

"That's for Bishop to decide," said Haze.

"I'll think about it," grunted Karstetter.

"Do it," said Haze, more intense than Karstetter had ever seen him. "Pass it on, quickly. Don't miss out, for crissake."

"I'll see," said Karstetter noncommittally.

He was still looking unhappy after Haze had gone.

A doubt kept gnawing at him. Was the other side using them? Was Galov a setup?

Was Haze . . . ?

Half an hour later a most-urgent top-secret message began to be sent to Washington, in the "Eyes Only" code that was strictly for Bishop's use.

Frankfurt

"Doesn't he look smart?" said Shura proudly, passing over to Nicolai the color photo of her brother.

It showed a young man in the walking-out uniform of a Red Army lieutenant, posing self-consciously for the camera. Raya, her young brother, was twenty-two, and had just been commissioned, after spending three years in officer school.

"Papa hopes he'll go on to the Frunze academy," said Shura. "He came in fourth in his group."

Papa's rank as staff colonel couldn't do any harm either, thought Nicolai cynically. He looked more closely at the red tabs, but he couldn't make out the service branch insignia.

"What section is he going into?" he asked.

"Raya wants to serve with the rocket troops, but with the high grades he had in the Suvorov seminary, and then as an officer cadet, maybe he'll go into something special." Shura nodded complacently at the thought, and added: "He really is very bright, and I'm not just saying it because I'm his sister."

Something special? The army political commissariat? The GRU? Even . . .

"An officer's uniform becomes him," said Shura, taking back the photo. "He's very handsome. And do you know, he speaks English perfectly now. Almost as good as you, so Papa says."

"So he'll probably end up on the Chinese border," grunted Nicolai. "And if he spoke Chinese, they'd station him in Poland. You know military bureaucracy. It's almost as bad as ours."

"That's not true." Shura was quite indignant. She was an army child, born, raised, and educated in the Red Army ambience, and antimilitary sentiments were blasphemy.

Nicolai shrugged.

"Anyway, you didn't do so badly," said Shura. "Straight from military service into the KGB. They found the right niche for you."

"Did they?" Nicolai smiled. "I'm glad you think so."

"You've got nothing to complain about, Nicolai." It was like a schoolteacher's reprimand.

He had brought Shura to one of Frankfurt's smartest restaurants, and they sat at a discreet table in an alcove. It had been a long time since he had taken her out, and she was both puzzled and pleased.

She reached for his hand across the table. "You're not really happy here, are you, darling?" Her green eyes were sympathetic. "I can understand it. Germany!" She made a grimace. "Who could like it? I feel like you about this place." She squeezed his hand. "We've been here two years, why don't you ask for a new posting?"

"It doesn't work like that, and you know it. They decide where one goes. And when. And why."

"Your English is so good, they're bound to find you useful in London or in America," continued Shura.

"It's not up to me."

"Well, at least we can take some leave back home," said Shura. "They owe you a lot of furlough. I think you're due at least three months. We could have a month on the Black Sea by ourselves and spend the rest of the time with my family. You can visit your mother and we can be free as larks. No duty, no pressures, no secrets."

"No." His voice was firm.

Shura's pretty face clouded over. "Why on earth not? You're entitled to it. And I could do with time away from these ugly Germans." She paused. "Don't you miss home?"

"Of course I do," but it sounded hollow. "It's just not . . . it's not the right time. There's too much to do here. I can't leave Rostov on his own. He's . . . he hasn't had a chance to settle in."

Her eyes were sad. "What is wrong?" she whispered. He had withdrawn his hand, and now he clenched it so hard the knuckles showed white.

"You keep asking what's wrong," he almost snapped. "Nothing is wrong, do you understand? Nothing, nothing. Don't ask stupid questions." He broke off, like a man who's realized that he's nearly lost his temper.

"Are you bored with me?" asked Shura. Her lips did not tremble, there were no tears in her eyes. She was a soldier's daughter. But she could not hide her anxiety.

"What a stupid thing to say," said Nicolai. "How could I be bored by you, babushka? Would I take you out if I were bored?" He sighed. "I know it is not easy for you. I leave you on your own a lot, I go out in the evenings, I am away for days. But it is only because I have to. It is for the department. It is my duty. You know I cannot tell you everything."

"I only wish you could tell me something," murmured Shura. "Sometimes lately it's been like living with a stranger. You have lost interest in me as a person and," she swallowed, "as a woman."

"Listen," he said. He waited till the white-aproned waiter had passed. "There is something big on. Very important, very secret. The biggest thing I have ever done. But I cannot say a word. You must understand. It is on my mind the whole time, every minute. If I neglect you, forgive me. One day you will know why. . . ."

She mouthed a little kiss at him. "I didn't know. I had no idea. It all seemed so routine. Now I see. Don't worry. I won't say anything anymore. Now you've explained."

But her green eyes had become alert, wary. Or perhaps they were suspicious.

They left the restaurant together, a handsome married couple, going home after a pleasant dinner out.

Haze sat at a corner table by himself, and as they passed he was reading the *Frankfurter Allgemeine*. He glanced up, gave Nicolai a smile, and went back to his paper. If Shura noticed, she said nothing.

Nicolai held open the Volkswagen door for Shura, got in himself, and they drove off. The black Mercedes parked nearby waited for a few moments, then started to follow at a respectful distance.

Washington

One after the other, the slides were flashed on the screen. They were all photographs of Nicolai Galov, some blurred, some quite crystal clear, some taken with telephoto lenses, some quite close up. They had all been surreptitiously shot in Frankfurt.

There was Nicolai leaving the consulate in the Beethovenstrasse, walking alongside the green houses in the Palmengarten, window-shopping in the Rossmarkt, or just strolling.

There was only one snapshot of Nicolai in the company of Shura, getting out of the Volkswagen.

"Who's that?" asked the Admiral in the darkness.

"That's his wife," explained Bishop.

"Not bad-looking," commented the Admiral. "A little hard maybe, but look who she married. How come we haven't got more pictures of her?"

"Well," said Bishop, "they don't appear to spend much time together, and she keeps to herself. Anyway, she isn't the target, is she?"

The lights came on, and the Admiral asked: "Do they

get on? Is everything lovey-dovey, or do they have a problem?"

"You show me a marriage that doesn't have a problem." Bishop's smile was twisted.

"Stow the cynicism, Carl." Inwardly, the Admiral wondered about Bishop's home life. He couldn't remember whether he was married or not, or living with somebody, or . . . Ah well, personnel would have his file. Aloud, he said: "That could be a useful pointer, don't you agree? If his marriage was all washed up. Could explain why he wants to get out."

The Admiral was a comparative newcomer to the intelligence world; he had been brought in because he had clean hands, hadn't been involved in any of the old nastiness, and had distinguished himself as a task-force flag officer off Vietnam. But his naïveté about covert intelligence operations made Bishop cringe at times.

"Sir," he said gently enough, "I don't believe their people turn defector because their domestic situation is fucked up any more than ours do."

"Don't ours, sometimes?" asked the Admiral, apparently innocently, and it reminded Bishop that the man wasn't *all* that naïve.

"Anyway, Admiral, you've seen the pictures. He doesn't seem to have noticed we were taking them, or if he did he apparently couldn't care less."

"Anything else?" asked the Admiral.

"We're keeping tabs on him. The German security people naturally have their eye on the consulate in any case, purely routine, but we're doing our own watch. Not that we've found out much about our friend."

"Which of course shows how smart the guy is if he is planning to come over. He doesn't want to attract his own people's attention, either, does he?"

For a moment, they were both silent. The Admiral had started doodling.

"You want to pursue this?" asked Bishop.

"You bet," said the Admiral. "If it's possible to get him, we want him." He noted Bishop's reaction. "You disapprove, Carl?"

"No. I just think something is—oh, I don't know. You know me, Admiral. The born pessimist."

The Admiral was due at the National Security Council meeting, and his secretary had already placed the stack of classified files he would need on his desk. He was anxious to get going.

"Well, Carl, I think we ought to do some serious fishing. Let's get some bait out, and if he bites, reel him in. Okay?"

"Okay," said Bishop. "I'll do my best."

They both stood up.

"Got any idea what you're going to use for bait?"

"Oh yes," said Bishop. "Oh yes, indeed."

Phoenix

The man in the steel-framed glasses picked up his car at the airport and, half an hour later, drove into the grounds of the Arizona Biltmore. He had only one large leather holdall bag with him, which he carried into the hotel himself.

He had asked for one of the chalets, at the back of the main hotel building, and the pretty suntanned receptionist gave him the key.

"Have a nice stay, Mr. Fletcher," she said, flashing him a welcoming smile.

"I'm sure I will," said the man as she rang for a bellboy to carry his bag.

"Any golf clubs, sir?" asked the porter.

"Don't play golf," said the man.

The porter wheeled the trolley with the one piece of luggage through the lobby and out along the colonnade that led to the cluster of chalets standing by themselves.

"Here we are, sir," said the bellboy, opening the door with a passkey. He put the holdall down in the bed-sitting room. "Anything I can get you?" he asked.

"No thanks," said the man. He gave the bellboy a five-dollar tip.

"Thank *you*," said the bellboy, pleasantly surprised. For what he had had to carry, he hadn't expected much more than a dollar.

"Have a good day, sir," he said, and closed the door of the chalet.

The man went into the bathroom, switched on the light, and looked at himself in the mirror. His blue eyes examined the reflection with a kind of detached interest. He went back into the bedroom and opened the holdall. He took out a leather toilet bag, a couple of shirts, some underwear. He was traveling light; he knew it would not be a long stay.

An hour later the man the hotel knew as Mr. Fletcher drove out of the grounds, turned right, and followed the traffic in an easterly direction. Once he pulled off onto the shoulder of the road and sat behind the wheel, watching the other cars stream past. It was just to check if another car would also pull up alongside the road. But no one was tailing him.

The man switched on the car radio and drove on again. After a few miles, he reached the outskirts of Phoenix. The fringe of the desert was not far away, but he turned off the road and eventually stopped in front of a cabin with a garish sign that proclaimed MASSAGE, 24 HOURS A DAY. Another sign was nailed on the door: YOUNG GEISHA GIRLS.

The man opened the door of the cabin and pushed aside a bead curtain. Beyond, a swarthy woman sat in an armchair. The rest of the shack was partitioned off.

"Hi," said the woman. She had been reading a tattered, ancient copy of the *Ladies' Home Journal* and was drinking coffee from a paper cup.

"Open for business?" asked the man.

"Sure," said the woman.

"My name is Fletcher."

"From New York?" the woman inquired.

"Correct."

"Did you stop off anywhere?" asked the woman sharply, like somebody giving a cue to which there was only one correct answer.

"Kansas City. For twenty minutes."

The woman stood up. "Would you like a cup of coffee?" she said cordially. "It's only instant, but you're welcome." Her manner had become very friendly.

"No thanks," said the man. "I've got a tough schedule."

"Sure," said the woman.

She was wearing a bathrobe, and her legs were bare. She smelled of cheap perfume.

"Excuse me," she apologized, and disappeared behind a door in the partition.

He looked around the shack. It was very primitive, with a minimum of furniture. The place gave the impression of having been hastily nailed together from wooden crates.

The woman reappeared. "Here," she said, and handed him an envelope. "Just follow the map."

He took the envelope. "It checked out?" he asked.

"Dead right," she said.

He smiled. A nice way of putting it. "Well done," he said.

"My pleasure."

He left without another word, got into the car, and drove back to the Biltmore.

In his chalet, he locked the door. He sat on the bed, and unzipped the toilet bag. He took out a small cardboard box that contained six tiny little glass ampules.

From his pocket he produced a gold cigarette lighter. He unscrewed part of it and very carefully inserted one of the ampules into the cavity.

Then he turned the screw tight, laid the lighter on the bed, replaced the lid on the cardboard box, and put it back into the toilet bag.

He picked up the lighter. It was beautifully made, a fine piece of craftsmanship.

And it never failed him.

Frankfurt

Nicolai had just bought the *Herald Tribune* from the newsstand at the side of Paul's Kirche when he saw the woman.

She was tall, and her clothes had the casual style that hinted they had cost plenty. Her dark hair was ruffled by the wind and she wore the lightest of makeup. She was slim, long-legged, and very attractive.

She was holding a camera and trying to photograph the steeple of the church. Then she noticed that Nicolai was watching her.

"Do you know anything about photography?" she asked. She was American, but Nicolai knew that before she spoke. She had style, he decided, she had money, she was very self-possessed. And, yes, she really was very good-looking.

"Just a little," said Nicolai.

"Well, can you help me with this thing?" she pleaded. "I haven't got the hang of it. I'm not sure about the exposure. . . ."

"I think you'll find your camera will do it all for you," said Nicolai gently. "It's automatic."

"Oh," she said. "You're not American. . . ."

"Did you think I was?"

For a moment she looked confused. "Well, I guess I saw you buy the *Trib*. And you don't *look* German. I'm sorry."

"Don't worry about it," said Nicolai.

"And you're not English, either. . . ." she probed.

"I'm Russian," said Nicolai quietly.

"Good Lord," she said. She seemed to have forgotten all about the camera in her hands.

"Why, is that so strange?" he smiled.

She seemed slightly embarrassed. "No, of course not. It's just that . . . well, I guess I haven't met many Russians. I don't think I've ever met one. . . ."

"No tail, no horns, no fangs," said Nicolai mockingly. "Just like anybody else, believe me. Very human."

She slung the camera in its case around her shoulder.

"You must think me—terribly provincial," she said awkwardly.

Provincial was the last thing he would have called her. Sophisticated, yes, worldly, much-traveled. And certainly a lady who would know how to use the expensive camera she had.

"Not at all," said Nicolai courteously. "Tell me, are you going to take that picture?"

"I can do that anytime." She dismissed it carelessly. "I'm sorry to have bothered you . . ."

"But it's no bother," said Nicolai. He looked at his watch. "It's nearly lunchtime. How about a cocktail?"

Her eyes twinkled. "Are all Russians that fast?"

"I told you, we're very human," he said.

She smiled. "Where shall we go?"

"You know the Frankfurter Hof?" he asked.

"Why," she said, "I'm staying there."

"Now, that's a coincidence," said Nicolai.

"Yes." It came almost mockingly. "Isn't it?"

He liked her. He liked the way she played the game.

"Well, come on," he said. "What are we waiting for?"

In the cocktail lounge she said she'd like a martini. Very dry.

"I'll have the same," he told the waiter.

"What, no vodka?" Again, that mocking look.

"You've got a lot to learn about Russians," said Nicolai.

"I'm sure. And isn't it time you told me your name?"

"Nicolai Galov."

"And what do you do, Nick?" She called him Nick as if he were an old friend.

"First you tell me about yourself," said Nicolai.

"My name is Gail Howard. I live in Malibu. In California. I'm doing the big tourist thing. London, Paris, Rome. Now you know it all."

"And Frankfurt?"

"Castles on the Rhine. Heidelberg. The Lorelei. Couldn't miss those, could I?" The waiter brought the drinks, and she tasted her martini. She made a slight grimace. "I guess it's okay, for Deutschland. Cheers."

Was she on her own? he wondered. No husband? No boyfriend? There was no wedding ring, he noticed.

She reached forward and took a tiny pretzel from the glass dish on the table.

"But you still haven't told me what you're doing here," she complained. "I want to know. I don't like people who play mysterious."

He grinned. "Nothing mysterious. Very unglamorous, I'm afraid. I'm at our consulate here."

She opened her brown eyes wide. "You know, I don't believe it. I think you're . . ." She frowned like someone trying to find the right answer to a crossword clue. "I think you're much more sinister. I bet you're a real live spy. I've always wanted to meet one, and now that I have—"

"Gail, I'm sorry to disappoint you," said Nicolai regretfully. "Nothing that exciting. Just a paper-shuffler."

"I think you're a KGB man," she insisted mischievously. "Walking around Frankfurt and picking up unescorted American women tourists." She looked very happy. "Wait till I tell the folks back home. They'll never believe it. Cocktails with a Russian agent."

He studied her across the table. "How long are you going to be here, Gail?"

"As long as there are interesting things to see," she replied, and their eyes met.

"That's nice," said Nicolai. "Would you like to have dinner sometime?"

"Nick," she said, "I wondered when you were going to ask."

Chandler

The man who called himself Fletcher, on this occasion,
followed the highway to Tucson, but some miles out of
Phoenix he turned right, and soon after a road sign announced CHANDLER.

He drove past the yellow-painted high school, and
along the main street. Chandler was a small town, neat
but rural, stuck in the middle of nowhere. What a place
for Kravisky to end up in, thought the man. He almost
felt sorry for him, buried away in this one-horse Arizona
hole, with its few stores, its little local paper, its isolation.
Kravisky, who had in his time been stationed in Brussels
and in Stockholm, had been resident in charge of illegals
in Holland. So this was his reward, hidden away here in
the back of beyond.

Maybe, reflected the man in the steel-framed spectacles,
it was a fitting reward for treason. Maybe he should just
be left to rot here, with boredom and the desert as his
daily companions.

But he had his orders, and Kravisky's turn had come.

Then it was back to Phoenix, check out of the hotel,
turn in the car at the airport, and fly off. He had already
booked his flight.

The filling station he wanted was a mile out of
Chandler, on the way to Williams Air Force base. When
he came to it, it turned out to be a cluster of two huts and
one gasoline pump.

Was this the new life Kravisky had wanted; this the reward for betraying his motherland? Or was he so scared
that he had begged the Americans to be allowed to vanish into this backwater, pumping gasoline into the cars of
farmers and small-town grocers?

It was hot, in the high nineties, and the road surface
shimmered. He wanted a cold drink, but that had to wait.
He slowed down, his cold blue eyes reconnoitering the
filling station.

Nobody was around. It seemed a good moment.

He pulled up in front of the single pump. Nobody came

out from either of the two huts. One appeared to be a store shed, the other some kind of ramshackle office.

The man sounded his horn. The sun was burning his eyes, and he had put on a pair of dark glasses.

Then the shuffling figure emerged. A man in oil-stained overalls. The photograph he had was twelve years old, but there was no doubt that this was Kravisky. Older, grayer, stooped. But Kravisky.

"Fill her up," ordered the man.

"Sure," said Kravisky who, according to the faded board with the peeling paint, now called himself JAKE BROWN (PROP.).

The man got out of the car and stretched himself.

"Not very busy, is it?" he said.

"Never is," said Kravisky alias Brown. His Ukrainian accent was barely detectable, and yet the three words he had said had a foreign sound.

The man watched as Kravisky fed the pipe into his tank.

"That'll be eight-fifty," said Kravisky, when the tank was full.

The man produced a fifty-dollar bill.

"You got anything smaller?" asked Kravisky wearily.

"Sorry," said the man. He pulled out a pack of cigarettes, stuck one in his mouth. Then he brought out the lighter.

"No smoking," said Kravisky sharply. "Can't you see the sign?"

"Sure I see it," said the man.

"I'll get your change," muttered Kravisky. He went into the hut, and the man followed him.

Inside, Kravisky unlocked a drawer and took out a tin box. He unlocked that and began counting out the change.

The man raised his lighter to the cigarette. He was standing close to Kravisky.

"I told you, no smoking," snapped Kravisky.

"My apologies, Major," said the man, and pressed the lighter. The vapor went straight into Kravisky's open-mouthed face; he inhaled enough to die in fifteen seconds.

He kneeled over and sprawled across the floor, his eyes unseeing.

"Dah Avidaiyah," said the man. He reached over and picked up his fifty-dollar bill.

Outside, a truck was passing on the road, but otherwise no one was around.

It was two hours before a motorist, wanting some gas, found the body of the man Chandler had known as Jake Brown.

Washington

Bishop sat in the one armchair in his office, his legs propped up on his desk. He allowed himself such informality only when no one would see him. He had given orders he was not to be disturbed.

He was reading through the Profile again. It was a bound file, the only copy in existence, and it recorded everything that was known to the United States about Nicolai Galov, vice consul of the U.S.S.R. in Frankfurt. Many sources had contributed to the Profile—the State Department, the CIA, foreign intelligence services, informers, newsmen, secret contacts. They had knowingly and unknowingly provided jigsaw pieces that now made up the dossier.

Bishop had ordered compilation of the Profile the way a general orders photo reconnaissance pictures of an enemy position. Somewhere in front of his eyes might be a hint, a clue, information others had missed—if only he looked hard enough.

The U.S. Embassy in Moscow had provided the information that Galov, as far as they knew, was born around 1942, "probably" in Moscow.

So you're about thirty-seven, Bishop thought to himself. For the umpteenth time he looked at the photograph of Galov on the second page of the Profile. It was the best one they had of him and it showed a very pleasant man; a handsome, youthful face with deepset eyes, topped by a mass of curly hair. His mouth had the hint of an amused smile, and Bishop registered that Galov probably had a sense of humor. That made him dangerous. Experience had taught Bishop that enemy agents who had humor were the trickiest.

The Moscow resident had found out that Galov's father, Lieutenant-Captain Piotr Galov, was killed in World War II, commanding the Soviet submarine *Katyushas* in the Baltic. This made young Nicolai a privileged child of the state.

Young Galov became a stalwart of the Komsomol, the

Communist Party youth organization. He must have been bright, for he was one of the fifteen successful candidates out of six hundred to enter the Institute of International Relations.

Bishop smiled. It was a nice euphemism for the KGB's elite academy for its top-grade agents, the ones who were intended to enter the higher echelons abroad.

As far as was known, added the Moscow contribution, Galov's only surviving family was his mother, aged sixty-seven. As the widow of an officer killed in action in the Great Patriotic War, and the mother of a KGB officer, she had a good apartment in Moscow, with no less than two rooms, a kitchen, and a bathroom to herself. A privilege for an elderly widow.

"Yes, sir," agreed Bishop to himself, "he *is* important."

The Moscow resident had added some personal comment:

Indications from all sources confirm that subject is the new-style "liberated" breed of KGB operator, modern, outward-looking, groomed to be poised and sophisticated, and to move with ease in Western circles. Unlike the taciturn, suspicious, and withdrawn old-style KGB man, Galov has great personal charm, does not indulge in dialectical jargon, and readily makes friends.

Bishop turned to the page headed "Personal Traits":

Subject dresses well and prefers Western clothes. He reads English for pleasure, and apparently has a subscription to *Playboy* magazine through the Soviet trading mission in the U.S.

He enjoys good food. He drinks martinis and whiskeys. He is a good driver. He likes the company of women and seems attracted to good-looking ones. He has been observed taking them out to expensive nightspots, and this has apparently not resulted in official disapproval from his superiors.

They were well informed, evidently, about Galov, thought Bishop, but vague about his real duties. Yet they knew enough to grade him highly dangerous.

The top-secret archive extract from Langley reported:

Galov is believed to be a counter intelligence officer of Special Service Section II of the 1st Chief Directorate. His section's missions apparently concentrate on:

1) Penetration of foreign security and intelligence services,

2) the supervisions of Soviet citizens abroad. This group covers Tass personnel, Aeroflot staff, trade representatives, diplomats, and exchange students.

3) close liaison with Department V, the Executive Action section, which covers physical action in the field, i.e., the blueprinting and carrying out of direct activities like assassinations, break-ins, sabotage, etc.

His mentor has been Vladimir Vasilevich Kirvoshey.

"Mentors" were supervisors who guided, advised, and watched the career of up-and-coming KGB stars. And Kirvoshey's name said a lot to Bishop. He had been the controller of Sergeant Lee Johnson, the GI traitor who had operated in the Armed Forces Courier Center in Berlin.

Bishop recalled with bitterness that Johnson, on the eve of giving Bishop some hitherto unexpected information, was murdered in 1972 in Lewisburg Penitentiary, where he was serving twenty-five years.

So Galov moved in those circles. . . .

The Profile was sketchy about Galov's actual postings. As far as they could make out, his first assignment abroad was as a junior attaché at the Soviet Consulate in Alexandria. He apparently spent six months in Athens but left very suddenly. A year later he was assigned to Vienna as a cultural attaché. A lengthy period followed in East Germany, on the staff of the Soviet political adviser. Then Frankfurt . . .

It was while in East Germany that Galov returned on leave to Moscow and married his wife.

"Shura, his wife, is the daughter of a Red Army staff colonel," said this section of the Profile, quoting information that had apparently reached Washington via the resident in Prague.

He was a key planner in the takeover of Czechoslovakia and is likely to be promoted to general very soon. Shura is a dedicated, loyal daughter of the Communist philosophy and state. Like her husband, she was a member of the Komsomol.

It is believed that she met her future husband when

Galov was temporarily assigned to KGB headquarters on Dzerzhinsky Street, where she worked for a time as a confidential secretary with the highest security clearance. Shura is a qualified pilot. She dislikes jazz.

Bishop raised his eyebrows. They *did* pick up the oddest scraps of information.

He got out of the armchair, went over to the flask on his desk, and poured himself a cup of coffee. He would like to meet Galov, he reflected.

He looked at his watch. It was 2 P.M. in Washington. In Frankfurt, it would be evening. In Moscow . . .

Was there somebody in Moscow, he wondered, reading his own dossier. Trying to piece together what made him tick. Trying to analyze what sort of opponent he was in this chess game they were playing. Trying to work out how he would assess Nicolai Galov.

Or were they, as yet, quite unaware of Galov's intentions?

Bishop sat down again and turned to the psychiatrist's evaluation of Galov. Not that Bishop had much faith in the psychiatrists who were now part of the agency's official analysis team. Dr. Harmer, who had been one of the very few people to be allowed sight of the Profile, wrote:

This subject is obviously a very intelligent man and, judging by his assignment, highly responsible and trustworthy. I am not in possession of enough information to make a thorough analysis, but I would judge that subject is a loyal, dedicated patriot, and a completely devoted member of his service. He belongs to the privileged class in the Soviet Union and has no cause to have any grievance against the service or the system. From the time he was a baby, he has had the best of education, housing, and recreation, all provided by the state.

However, it is possible that a man who is so "Westernized" in his person as subject appears to be may have become enamored of the West, and find himself longing for the material (rather than spiritual) benefits of the United States.

I would also judge that if subject has a weakness, it seems to be his fondness for attractive women. I wonder if his marriage is, possibly, one into which he entered because it is the perfect "state" marriage. I am not suggesting there is no attraction between the two, but simply that a man as ambitious (probably) and shrewd as Galov may have considered the advantages of marrying a senior Red Army officer's daughter, and a girl who obviously has KGB connections.

This leads one to wonder if subject's achilles heel is not his weakness for a pretty face. It may of course be an oversimplification to put it like that, but basically it is the only chink I can even suspect in his armor.

Ten minutes later, the yellow phone, which was secure, could not be tapped, and connected him direct to the operations room, buzzed, and they told him that another one was dead. In a little hick town called Chandler, in Arizona.

The Rhine

They leaned against the railings of the tourist steamer as it moved slowly along the river. She was staring straight ahead, and her clear-cut profile somehow made her seem a little harder. But again, the wind ruffled her hair the way he liked so much, and he just thought of her as a woman, and nothing else. . . .

For the moment.

"The other night . . ." he began.

"The other night was lovely, Nick," said Gail.

"I don't know what the maid must have thought," he grinned.

She turned her face to him. "Do you care?"

"Hell, no," said Nicolai.

"What about your people?" asked Gail.

His eyes hardened. "My people?"

"Don't they watch you? Won't there be reports, questions?"

"What reports?"

"I thought Russian diplomats are watched all the time. I mean, don't they know if you spend the night. . . ."

"Such talk is nonsense," said Nicolai. "Do you think they really could, even if they wanted to? Work it out yourself. It takes eight people to keep a complete twenty-four-hour surveillance on somebody. *Eight*. Not counting telephone monitoring. If you want to watch fifty people around the clock, you need over four hundred shadows. Where do you think our little consulate in Frankfurt would get four hundred shadowers from?" He laughed.

"You seem to know all about it," said Gail.

A barge flying Dutch colors slowly chugged past them, and their steamer gave it a friendly blast on its siren.

"I think it is so funny, the picture people have," said Nicolai. "They think the gardener is a colonel in the secret police, and the chauffeur is a master spy. The ambassador cringes because the chef in the kitchen is the political commissar. The TV antenna on the roof sends secret code messages, of course, and if we give a party, the vodka is drugged, the cigarettes are doped, and the picture on the wall is bugged. And while you hang up your coat, somebody takes your photo secretly. It's so ridiculous."

"Isn't any of it true?" asked Gail innocently.

"You've been reading the wrong newspapers," he replied, and it was the first time she had heard him voice a party-line statement that sounded like a cliché out of the official textbook.

"I'm cold," said Gail. "Let's go downstairs."

They descended into the saloon and found a table by a window, overlooking the river and the slowly passing shore.

"I'd like a brandy," said Gail when the waiter came.

"Coffee," ordered Nicolai.

She grimaced. "How boring, Nick."

"I try to keep a clear head when I talk business," said Nicolai.

It took a second to sink in. Then her eyes narrowed. "What do you mean?" she asked very quietly.

"I've become very fond of you, Gail." He paused. "Much too fond of you in a few days. Sometimes I almost forget that you are an American agent. That you picked me up very neatly by accident on purpose. That I am your assignment."

"Nick . . ." she began.

He held up his hand. "Please. What is it that they say in the bad movies, don't let us spoil it. Let us accept the fact that I know who you are, and why you are here. . . ."

The waiter brought her brandy and set coffee in front of Nicolai.

"And let us accept the fact also," added Nicolai after the waiter had gone, "that I like you very much."

Very slowly she took a sip of brandy. "Really?" she said at last, putting down the glass.

"It means a lot that you know I am an operative of the KGB, and that I may have dropped some hints, and they may have been picked up, and you are here now on behalf of the CIA to . . . pursue the matter."

He unwrapped two lumps of sugar and dropped them into his coffee.

"Oh?" Her voice was cold.

"It has become important to me that there should be absolute truth between us," said Nicolai. "After all, my life depends on it. And also . . ."

"Yes?"

He smiled a little bitterly. "Is that not enough? My life?"

"Aren't you taking a hell of a risk, Nick, talking like this?" she asked. "How do you know you can trust me?"

He stirred the coffee. "I told you, I know who you are and what you are. Of course that doesn't mean I can trust you, I agree. But you see, I do. I look into your eyes, and I know I can trust you." He shook his head. "How stupid that sounds. I would have been thrown out of training school for such idiotic reasoning."

"It *is* idiotic," she agreed. But her voice was soft.

"In our business it is all planning and calculating, but sometimes one must take a chance. Sometimes, against all odds, one must trust."

"Yes, Nick," she said, "but can I trust you?" She corrected herself. "Can we trust you?"

He shrugged. "That's up to you. I've told you where I stand. I'm taking the risk. More than you."

"I don't know about that," she said in a low voice. "That's where you may be wrong."

A couple came over and beamed at them. The man, burly, round-faced, with a Tyrolean hunter's hat and a fox brush in the band, said: *"Bitte?"*

They stared at him, and at the buxom woman in the fur coat beside him.

"Koennen wir sietzen?" asked the man, and without waiting for an answer the two sat down at their table.

"We're going," said Nicolai in German, and nodded to the waiter. He paid the check, and they both went up on deck. Both were silent. And their time was up; the steamer was just pulling into Frankfurt.

Gail turned to him.

"Nick," she said urgently. "Don't do anything. Give me a call the day after tomorrow. But don't do anything until then."

"We've got a lot to talk about," he said.

"Not yet," she replied, and it sounded like a warning. She turned and walked away from him.

After the steamer had moored, they came off it separately. Gail suddenly didn't appear to want him around. He watched her hail a cab and drive off. She hadn't once looked back at him.

In his mind, Nicolai went over what he had said to her, and the way he had said it.

He wondered suddenly if he hadn't blown the whole thing.

Munich

As soon as Washington advised him that a woman operative had been assigned to "develop" Nicolai, Karstetter had wondered what sort of person she would turn out to be.

He had great respect for Bishop, whom he regarded as one of the agency's last real professionals, but he was surprised that Bishop had picked a woman. Karstetter was chauvinistic about his profession. He accepted the fact that times had changed. Sure, there were now women judges and women jockeys, female stevedores and female boxers, women ambassadors and lady cops.

But in his view, women had a subsidiary role in intelligence work. Of course, the Mata Haris of the business, the temptresses, whose battleground was the bed into which they lured the enemy, played a key part. But who the hell had heard of a woman station chief, a woman resident? Or even a woman case officer in the field?

Bishop must have his reasons, but he tried to sort out, in vain, what they were.

Now Gail sat in front of him, after flying in from Frankfurt. In the pecking order, she had to report to him. Contact with the U.S. Consulate in Frankfurt, and its agency people there, was to be avoided. He was the go-between with Bishop.

"So you're getting on with him?" said Karstetter, somewhat drily. His instinct told him that Gail seemed to regard Nicolai not as the mere subject of the exercise; that she thought of him as a person. It was always bad news when the surgeon had a liking for the man he was going to cut up; it could cause complications.

"I think we should go ahead," replied Gail coolly. "The word hasn't been mentioned once, but I believe he wants to come over."

"What word hasn't been mentioned?" asked Karstetter sharply.

"Defection."

"Then—"

"We speak in a different kind of language," she interrupted. "Anyway, he's put his cards on the table."

She put her hand in her smart, expensive handbag and brought out a small cassette.

"Listen for yourself," she said.

Karstetter took a small tape recorder out of the right-hand drawer of his desk, fitted in the cassette, and pressed the play button.

"I try to keep a clear head when I talk business," came Nicolai's voice. Karstetter listened intently to the rest of the tape, while Gail watched him, smoking a cigarette.

At the end, he switched off. "Tell me," he said, "did you record everything?"

She blew out a cloud of smoke. "All the relevant parts."

"Hmm. He does say that he has become very fond of you. . . ."

"Well, that's my assignment, isn't it?" Gail said shortly.

"You've been out together, haven't you?" asked Karstetter. As a young G2 lieutenant in Korea, he had been an excellent interrogator. "Isn't he taking a heck of a risk? Frankfurt is a small place, really. His people may also know what you are, and if they see him all cozy with you, surely—"

"He doesn't seem bothered," said Gail.

"Maybe he isn't because *you*, honey, are *his* assignment."

Gail bristled. She didn't like being called honey. And she didn't like his slightly patronizing tone. "I don't believe so," she said curtly. "And I think he's smart enough to know what he's doing and how to do it."

Karstetter looked resigned. After all, she was Bishop's choice. "Well, it's up to the big boys, isn't it?" he said amiably. "You want me to indicate that so far things look positive. . . ."

"I want you to tell them to start preparing the contingency plan," she ordered crisply. "I think he will go through with it, and pretty soon we're going to have to lift a defector. So let's be ready."

"What about his wife?"

"Well?"

"Have you discussed it with him?" said Karstetter. "Do you think he wants her to come with him?"

"I don't believe so." Gail's voice was flat.

"That won't do, Mrs. Howard." He was very official and formal now. "How can we plan a lift if we don't know how many are coming?"

"I don't believe they're very close," said Gail. "But of course, I'll make sure."

"And let me know fast. Should we decide to go ahead." She nodded.

Karstetter cleared his throat. "Your report is much appreciated, and I'll inform the section. Bishop is waiting for a situation assessment from you, and I'll see that he has it pronto."

"Thank you," said Gail.

He dropped his official demeanor. "Listen, why don't you stay overnight? There is a spare room at the house, and you're very welcome. If you don't mind being woken up every three hours, that is. We have a new baby, but I know my wife would love . . ."

She looked grateful but shook her head. "I've got the return flight booked. The sooner I'm back in Frankfurt, the better. . . . But I do appreciate the offer, believe me."

"Some other time," said Karstetter politely.

He hesitated as she got her things together, and then took the plunge. "Do you mind if I ask you something personal? There's strictly no need for me to know, but Bishop didn't tell me much about you. How come you're in the company?"

She stood up and faced him, reacting to the service jargon. "It's very simple," she said dispassionately. "My husband was a Navy flyer. He went down over Vietnam. I couldn't live with memories forever. I tried but it didn't work. My family knew somebody who . . . well, here I am."

"It can be dangerous work, Gail," said Karstetter sincerely.

"War is dangerous, Jack," she said quietly.

"And you are fighting your own?"

"Perhaps," she said.

"This work we do . . ." he began, but she cut him short, impatiently.

"This work," she cried, "is the best way I know to get back at the bastards."

After she had gone, he was still a little aghast at the vehemence with which she'd spoken.

He put the cassette in the safe. He would have liked to hear the full tape. He wondered if she had kept it running even while she made love with one of the bastards she hated so much.

Frankfurt

Shura was a quarter of an hour early at the Café am Opernplatz, and she sat down at a table that gave her a good view of anybody who came in. She smoked nervously, and every time somebody entered she looked up eagerly and sat back disappointed when it didn't turn out to be the person she was waiting for.

Then the Mercedes cab pulled up and Rostov got out. He spotted her immediately as he came through the glass doors, and went over to her table, beaming.

"My dear Shura," he greeted her. "Sorry I'm so late. I was held up at the consulate."

He bent down and kissed her on both cheeks, very paternally.

"Have you been waiting long?" he asked anxiously as he sat down.

"It doesn't matter," said Shura. "It doesn't matter at all now you're here, dear Ivan Ivanovitch. I've been so looking forward to this."

"So have I, so have I," rumbled Rostov genially. He noted her empty cup. "You will have another coffee? Good."

He ordered it from the pert waitress with the lace apron.

"And a pot of hot chocolate for me, with thick whipped

cream," he added. Guiltily, he confessed to Shura: "It is my great weakness. You won't tell, will you?"

She looks pale, he thought, her face is drawn, anxious. But aloud he said: "You look as beautiful as ever. Nicolai is a lucky fellow. . . ."

Shura smiled wanly. "What a long time it has been," she said. "You must tell me all the news. How is my father?"

"The colonel sends you his love. He says you don't write enough. It doesn't cost you anything, you can use the diplomatic pouch, he says, so why don't you write more?"

He broached the next subject delicately. "I too have a bone to pick with you, dear Shura. Why haven't you invited me to your home? Why have I not seen you since I arrived in Frankfurt? Why are you avoiding me?"

The waitress brought them their hot drinks on a silver tray. Rostov got the customary little glass of mineral water with his chocolate.

He was pleased. "So civilized. The Germans have some good qualities at least." He became serious again. "Well, Shura? What's wrong, dear?"

She slipped off her wolf-fur jacket. It was getting too warm in the well-heated café.

"Why should anything be wrong?" she asked, and it sounded so artificial she almost went red.

"I have been a friend of your family for too long," said Rostov. "I know when something isn't right. Why meet here and not in your home? We are not lovers who have to sneak into hidden corners to avoid being seen. Why have you been avoiding me?"

She looked at him gravely.

"I'm worried about Nicolai," she said.

"Ah. Nicolai." His eyes flickered. "What's the matter with him?"

Suddenly the floodgates opened. "Ivan Ivanovitch," Shura burst out, "you know I'm a good wife. You know I don't complain. I understand Nicolai's work—your work. I understand the long hours, and that men doing your job can't talk much, not even to their families, and that everything must take second place to one's duty. I know it and I respect it, but . . ."

"What are you trying to tell me?"

Shura stubbed out her almost unsmoked cigarette. There were already five in the ashtray.

"Please," she begged. "I must ask you something I

42

shouldn't. Is—is Nicolai working on something . . . something special? Is he on a very big mission here?"

"Shura, you know I can't answer a question like that," Rostov said gently.

"Please," she repeated. "It would explain so much. It would put my heart at ease. He's hinted that he's on something very big—'the biggest thing I have ever done.' That's all he let slip."

"There you are, then," said Rostov. "He's given you the answer."

"But is he really?" Shura demanded almost desperately.

"Why is it so important to you?" Rostov frowned. "You sound as if you don't believe him. What does it matter to you?"

"It would explain so much." She twisted her hands in her lap. "Nicolai has been so—so strange. For a long time now. I don't think it's anything to do with his work. A woman senses these things. A wife especially. No, he has something else on his mind. He has become remote, distant, cold. He is preoccupied every minute. He shuts me out. He wants no contact. He knows you're a family friend, but he has tried to prevent a meeting between us. He is anxious but he refuses to talk about taking leave. It is not only his work that is secret to me. *He* has become a secret."

"My poor Shura," said Rostov. He looked worried. "Are you sure you're not just imagining things?"

But Shura just went on: "I started wondering if it is another woman. He has been out all night twice."

Rostov sat very still.

"He acted so strange I really started to suspect he was having an affair. I even thought I saw him with a woman. A very smart woman. In the Hauptwache. Last Wednesday. But I may have been wrong. It could have been another couple."

"Go on," said Rostov.

"I could have asked him, I suppose, but there is a brick wall between us. Yet I don't really think it is another woman. . . ."

"Intuition again?"

"I don't know." She paused. "But I am afraid."

"He has been working very hard," Rostov began soothingly. "But I can assure you his work is satisfactory. After all, I am his superior and I should know. Since I have arrived at this post, I have made it my business to keep my eye on a lot of things. Including Nicolai. So don't worry."

"I have had a terrible suspicion growing in me, and I haven't known what to do about it," said Shura. She stared into Rostov's eyes. "You know I am not disloyal. To my husband." Her voice lowered. "Or to my homeland."

"What are you trying to say?" Rostov asked very gently.

"Ivan Ivanovitch, there is no one else I can turn to, no one to whom I can say my innermost thoughts. No one I can speak to about my fears. I talk to you not as an officer of the service, not as Nicolai's superior, but as a friend. A friend of the family."

"Of course."

She fell silent and contemplated the table, avoiding facing him.

"You still haven't told me what it is you are afraid of," Rostov reminded her.

"Perhaps I shouldn't say a thing, but my father is a soldier and I know what he would do. Above all, above people, above relationships is our country. Is that not so?"

Rostov nodded.

"It is the most terrible choice a woman has to face, but—"

"But duty is our obligation," Rostov prompted softly.

She had tears in her eyes as she said: "I love Nicolai so. I don't want to lose him. Perhaps . . . this way . . ." She swallowed. "Perhaps this way you can still save him. . . ." A tear trickled down her cheek.

Rostov waited.

"I think . . ." Shura said with difficulty, "I believe Nicolai is thinking of defecting."

"I know he is," said Rostov.

Frankfurt

Nicolai called her hotel from a phone booth and asked for her room. It was in the middle of the afternoon, but she answered. He wondered if she had stayed in especially to wait for him to call.

"Where are you speaking from?" she asked. It was the first time she seemed concerned about security.

"A phone booth," said Nicolai. "You didn't expect I'd

call from—" He nearly said "the consulate," but instead changed it to: "From my place, did you?"

"Everything all right?" she asked.

"Sure," he said.

"Good."

"How was the trip?" he asked.

"What trip?"

"Munich."

There was silence at the other end. She wanted to ask him how he knew about Munich, what he knew. But instead she said: "I think we ought to meet."

"How about dinner?" suggested Nicolai.

"Somewhere discreet?"

"I know a place," he said. "It's just across the river, on the other side. Sachsenhausen. The old part of Frankfurt. Have you been?"

"No."

"Let's meet at the Schwarze Zwerg. It's a little dive in a cellar. Take a cab to the Brueckenstrasse, walk down an alley called the Graf Gasse, and you'll see it on the left-hand side. I'll be there at eight."

"It *is* discreet?" she insisted.

"Listen," said Nicolai, "it's so small there are only four or five tables, and you can see every soul who goes in or out. And it's so out of the way that even the police can't find it. It's discreet, all right."

"Okay," she said. "I'll be there."

"Is . . . is everything all right?" he asked. For some reason, he was uneasy.

"I'll see you at eight," she said, and hung up.

He came out of the phone booth and looked around. He had no shadow. He was sure of that.

Sachsenhausen

Gail paid off the cab and looked for the Graf Gasse. Sachsenhausen was quite different from the other half of Frankfurt, across the Main River. It was medieval, small, with mazes of alleyways and cul-de-sacs.

She walked in the wrong direction at first, but then retraced her steps. Nicolai had given her the impression that once she was in the Brueckenstrasse, it would be easy to find the Graf Gasse, but already she was late and still hadn't located it.

She saw a man strolling along, and not till she had stopped him did she realize he was Turk or a Cypriot.

"Graf Gasse?" she smiled hopefully, but he gave her a grin, revealing broken, yellowed teeth, then shook his head and walked on.

She stopped another passerby.

"Wo ist die Graf Gasse, bitte?" asked Gail in her tourist German.

"Da oben," said the man curtly, pointing to a narrow dark passageway between two old houses. His manner was highly disapproving; evidently nice women did not inquire after that place at this time in the evening.

Gail entered the passageway. The alley was much longer than she had expected, and she started following it. She still hadn't spotted the place. She had imagined there'd be a neon sign, or some kind of illumination. Wherever it was in this gloomy, dark alley it didn't exactly advertise itself. Discreet, Nick had said. This joint, she thought, was positively reticent.

She was halfway up the long alley when she began to feel a curious sense of entrapment. She glanced around, but nobody was following her; she would have heard footsteps anyway. Normally, she was not a nervous person, but this was a place she'd rather not be in.

Now the alley was broadening out slightly, and doorways began to appear. She felt more confident, and then she saw a small lamp hanging over some stone steps leading down into a basement. She could just distinguish the gothic lettering: *Zum Schwartzen Zwerg.* "At the Black Dwarf."

Nick certainly knew some curious places in odd corners. But then, so did all KGB men.

She stiffened. She had an acute feeling of danger. It wasn't the unease that she'd previously sensed, when she started walking along the Graf Gasse. This was a full-blown alert.

She hesitated. The steps down into the basement were just ahead of her. Everything seemed deserted. And yet . . .

Then she saw a movement in the shadows, and almost simultaneously she heard the shot. Despite her panic, she remained amazingly in control of her reaction. She melted into a doorway, just as the dark figure emerged. He started walking toward her. She was trapped. There was another shot, and she felt a bullet strike the wall a few inches from her.

Gail crouched, and when her hand emerged from her bag there was a small, compact automatic in it. Twice she fired at the figure, and she heard a cry. The shadow turned and started running toward the far end of the alley.

Gail stepped out of the doorway and fired again. This time she held her gun just as she had been taught at the firing range, with both hands, aiming calmly and deliberately at the retreating figure as it began to be swallowed up by the gloom.

The figure fell and then lay motionless on the cobbles of the alley. There was total silence. It was eerie.

"Never believe they're dead until you've made sure," the instructors had told her, and as she cautiously approached the body, her finger was on the trigger of her gun.

"Gail," somebody shouted, and she froze. She heard steps, and was about to swing around when an arm grabbed her.

"Get out of this, quick," cried Nicolai. "Run like hell."

He half-pushed, half-dragged her away from the body.

"Let go," she panted. "He may still be alive."

"Does it matter?" he snarled, and kept dragging her toward the exit of the Gasse. "We've got to get away before we're seen."

The sound of running feet was already echoing from the other end of the passageway.

They emerged into the Brueckenstrasse. She was still holding the gun in her hand, and as they stood breathless, she hastily put it into her bag.

"Now walk, don't run," instructed Nicolai.

He guided her around corners and up side streets until they emerged into a main road with traffic lights and cars and taller buildings.

They stopped outside a brightly lit shop window. He stared at her face, scrutinizing it like a man who had never really observed it properly.

"What the devil happened?" he demanded.

"Who was it who tried to kill me, Nick?" said Gail. It sounded almost accusing. "Your people?"

"Damn you, if I knew do you think I wouldn't have warned you? Somebody must have followed me," he snapped.

"How very careless of you. And why didn't you want me to see who it was?" she asked, not even trying to disguise her suspicion.

"So you could get caught by the German police? Do you think that would be wise?" he said curtly. "Anyway, he'd just be a face. It wouldn't mean anything. One dead man. He wouldn't exactly carry his biography in his pocket."

A taxi was approaching, and he waved it down. He held the door open for her.

"Frankfurter Hof," he told the driver.

"Aren't you coming?" asked Gail.

"You get back to the hotel," he said. "I've got a lot of thinking to do."

Through the rear window, she saw him walking back into the darkness of Sachsenhausen.

Washington

The face of the assassin stared up at Bishop. It lay on the desk in front of him, a photo-fit composite the FBI had proudly brought in.

It was amazingly accurate, though Bishop had no way of knowing that. The nose was not quite right, and the lips were a little too thin. The hairline was too low, but overall there was no mistaking him. Even the steel-framed glasses were right.

"The boys in Arizona have done a pretty good job," the deputy director of the FBI had said admiringly. And he was right.

"Jake Brown's" killing had set Chandler buzzing. So had the sight of the investigators who suddenly arrived in the little town in their dust-covered black cars. They weren't just state cops, but FBI men, and others, from agencies that didn't identify themselves.

They went around asking people questions, checking and cross-checking, and they found that somebody had noticed a car driven by a stranger. Strangers in Chandler were noticed. It was that sort of town.

No, they didn't recall the car's license-plate number, but the guy who drove it wore glasses. A kid outside the yellow school had had a very good look at him.

An FBI artist painstakingly fitted together various impressions of the stranger, concentrating on the features the three key witnesses seemed to agree on.

Once they had combed the little town, the agents established that the stranger hadn't stayed there, but only passed though. The net was spread farther out. It seemed possible he had come from Phoenix. They checked first the motels, then the small lodging houses and the cheap hotels, and drew a blank. The expensive places didn't yield any clues either. At first.

But at the Arizona Biltmore somebody remembered Mr. Fletcher. A receptionist recognized the rough drawing, and she added and confirmed other details. And the hotel had logged Mr. Fletcher's car license.

FBI men swarmed over the chalet the stranger had occupied for eighty dollars a night, much to the management's curiosity.

"What's he done?" they asked. "What do you want him for?"

"It's just routine," they smiled.

They found fingerprints in the chalet, but they were useless. Other people had moved in, and out again, and they couldn't pin anything down.

A waitress in the restaurant vaguely recalled Mr. Fletcher. She had helped him at the breakfast buffet, but he had asked for hot porridge.

"He said breakfast wasn't breakfast without his oats," she giggled. "It made me remember him."

The FBI men did not smile.

"Anything else you noticed about him?" one said encouragingly.

"No," she shook her head. "He looked like an ordinary guy. I thought he was a businessman. He was very polite. Oh yes. Wait a minute. His English was kind of foreign. . . ."

"An accent?"

"Not exactly." She didn't quite know how to put it. "Kind of precise. Clipped. He wasn't an American, maybe. From the East, I guess," she added.

They showed her the likeness.

"Hey, that's like him," she said. "I could swear . . . yes, pretty much like him."

They traced the car to the rental company at the Phoenix airport. He had paid cash. Nobody remembered his appearance, but the time of the car rental dovetailed with the arrival, ten minutes earlier, of a TWA jet from La Guardia via Kansas City.

It looked as if Mr. Fletcher might well have flown in from New York.

"And I guess is back there now," said the FBI man who handed Bishop the sheafs of witness statements and the completed photo-fit picture. "But that's as far as we can go at the moment."

"Well," said Bishop, "that's a hundred percent more than we had before."

"*If*, of course, he is the killer," cautioned the deputy director. "It isn't a crime to be a stranger in Chandler. Nobody saw him at the filling station, remember?"

"Well, I'll take a bet on it," said Bishop.

The deputy director raised his eyebrows.

"I feel it in my guts. It's him all right."

"We haven't got much to go on, really," insisted the deputy director.

"Oh, I wouldn't say that," said Bishop. "Clipped English, steel-framed glasses, and a yen for oatmeal at breakfast. You'd be surprised what the computer can come up with."

Moscow

The man in the fur hat rang the doorbell of the second-floor flat in the Moscow apartment building. He was fair-haired, with a moustache, and he waited patiently for somebody to answer.

The radio had been on in the apartment, but when the bell rang it was turned off. After a short while, the front door opened slightly. It was still on the chain.

An elderly, gray-haired woman peered through the gap. "Yes?"

"Natalia Galova?" said the man politely. "Please forgive the intrusion. I just want a few words with you. Major Zharnov. KGB." He smiled at her reassuringly.

"Come in, come in," said Nicolai's mother. She withdrew the chain and opened the door. "Please."

Zharnov entered the tiny hall. He took off his fur hat. "Thank you," he said.

"This way," said the old lady, leading him into the room she used as a parlor. "I wasn't expecting anyone, you must excuse the untidiness. But you're very welcome. It is always a pleasure to see one of Nicolai's comrades."

She was chattering away eagerly as she indicated for him to sit on the sofa by the window. She was an erect lady, straight as a ramrod, with her hair tightly held together in a bun. Her black wool dress was severe, but she wore an amber bead necklace.

"You're very kind," said Zharnov. He had taken off his overcoat. Despite his protests, the old lady insisted on hanging it up.

Zharnov glanced around the room, noticed the framed wedding photo of Nicolai and Shura. On the wall was another framed portrait, a man in a Red Navy officer's uniform. He guessed it was Nicolai's father, who had been killed in the war. Underneath was a glass case containing the ribbon and medal of a Hero of the Soviet Union.

"You will have some tea," said Nicolai's mother. The tea urn was already steaming in the corner, and she busied herself around it, then brought him a glass of black tea with a slice of lemon floating in it. "There," she said in a motherly fashion, "that will warm you up."

She sat down on the sofa beside him. "How kind of you to visit an old lady all on her own. Do you work with him? Are you one of his friends?" She was like a bright-eyed sparrow in her eagerness.

Zharnov put the glass of tea carefully on a mat on the table beside him.

"I don't actually know your son personally." He was half apologetic. "You must appreciate it is a very big organization. But I'm sorry I have never met him."

"Never mind, I'm sure you will one day," she said cheerfully. "But you have some news from him?"

"Do you mind if I smoke?" asked Zharnov.

"Please," said the old lady. "Make yourself at home."

He brought out a Russian cigarette with the long cardboard tube, and lit it with a Cartier lighter he had bought himself while on assignment in Paris.

"This is a very nice flat you have here, Natalia Galova," he said admiringly.

She drew herself up proudly.

"Yes. The state is very good to me. Both as a war widow and the mother of a public servant. But you haven't come to tell me that."

"No." He hesitated a second. "I just want to have a little chat about Nicolai."

She was puzzled. "I'm not quite sure I understand, Major—Major Zharnov. What about Nicolai . . . ?"

He picked his words carefully. "You must understand that we care about our people. We want to know that all is well with them and their families, especially when they are stationed abroad, doing important work. We have a duty to insure that they have no worries, and that they are happy."

"Of course," she said, but her manner was a little wary.

"Do you often hear from Nicolai?" he continued. "Does he write to you a lot? Does he keep in touch with you?"

"Why do you ask?" she said, rather stiffly. "Of course he does. He is a very good son. But why should you—the department—what has it to do with the KGB?"

"So may I ask if he has any problems?" said Zharnov carefully. "Do you know if anything worries him? Has he mentioned any . . . any unhappiness?"

She frowned. "Certainly not," she said curtly.

"Forgive me, but it is important. Do you think that perhaps his marriage . . ."

"What are you trying to say, Major?" demanded the old lady angrily. "I think this uncalled for. Why do you ask a thing like that? My daughter-in-law is a sweet child, he loves her very much, and so do I."

"Of course," said Zharnov quickly. "I told you our sole concern is his welfare. We only want to make quite certain that he is happy and has no worries."

"Why?" she snapped. She was no longer sweet and genteel, but hard.

"Your son's work is of the utmost importance to the state. He knows many secrets, and there can be no question of his being—well, in any way unreliable."

Suddenly her heart began beating heavily. The room had gone cold. His friendliness had turned mechanical. She had lived through the old days, through the Stalin era. She remembered the purges in the military. Their friends who had been arrested in the middle of the night. The officers who had been shot thirty minutes after a court-martial had sentenced them. The word "unreliable" had been only one step removed from the word "treason" in those days.

"Of course my son is reliable," she said, but the anger was defensive.

"No question of it," said Zharnov, but his smile seemed false to her. "You are his mother, however, and we feel that you would be the first to know if he was under any hostile . . . pressures. You would of course sense if he were discontented." She winced. Another of those words. "It is perfectly human to be restless sometimes, but in our work we cannot afford to be . . . too human. When a man is in Nicolai's position, there can be no doubts."

"What has happened?" she whispered.

The tea was growing cold, but he picked up the glass and drank a little.

"Nothing," he replied at last. "And we don't want anything to happen, do we?"

She was pale. "No," she said. "There is a reason. You would not come here and say these things—ask these questions—if you did not have a reason. . . ." Her eyes appealed to him. "What is wrong?"

Suddenly he was crisp, official. "The point is, Natalia Galova, that nothing must go wrong, and we rely on you to let us know if you have reason to believe that Nicolai might do something—unintelligent. It is your duty as a citizen, as the widow of a man who gave his life for his motherland, to inform us of anything that might be in the offing. Anything that makes you suspicious. It is in Nicolai's own interest. He may give you a hint of something, an indication. An odd word in a letter, a passing comment. You will tell us immediately. You understand?"

"But what is he suspected of?" she asked desperately.

He got up from the sofa. "We know we can rely on you," he said, ignoring her question. "After all, you owe a great debt to the state. You are in a highly privileged position. You have this lovely apartment. You have a generous pension. Everything you need. Special shopping facilities. It would be terrible to lose it all, would it not? You love Moscow. It would be so sad if an old lady like you found herself stuck in one room in some provincial hole, correct?"

He went over and took his coat off the peg. As he put it on, he suddenly switched on the charm. "But you must forgive me, Natalia Galova. All this is silly talk. We trust you implicitly. And remember, we are all very fond of Nicolai."

He fished out a card and gave it to her. "Two phone

numbers," he said. "Day and night. Whoever answers knows all about it. If you feel there is something we should be made aware of, call immediately."

Stiffly, like an automaton, she walked with him to the front door.

"Ah yes," he said, his glance sweeping around the hall. "This really is a very nice apartment. You are very lucky. Think of all the people who'd give their right hand to have it. . . ."

He put on his fur hat.

"My compliments, Natalia Galova."

He opened the front door himself and slammed it shut behind him.

She felt ice cold.

Washington

Karstetter received the summons after lunch, and next morning at breakfast time he reported to Bishop in Washington.

"Good flight?" asked Bishop, and that was the only reference he made to Karstetter's rush journey on priority travel orders.

They sat in the middle of the green-carpeted office, with a small table between them. On it was a tray with orange juice, toast, butter and jam, and coffee.

"Well, we got a name, Jack," announced Bishop. "Operation Pheasant."

"Who picked that one?" said Karstetter, not very enthusiastically.

"It was the next code name on the list. You should complain. One of the sections got Operation Gallbladder for a job in Greece. Anyway, there it is. Code word Pheasant for the lifting of Galov."

"It's definitely on?"

"All systems go. Orders from the top, National Security Council approval, and the blessing of our beloved Admiral."

"When?" asked Karstetter.

"ASAP. Since we're going to do it, the quicker the better."

"You happy about it, Carl?"

Bishop smiled sourly. "Have you ever known me to be happy about anything?"

"That's great. You know how to encourage a guy."

"I'm not here to raise our morale," said Bishop.

"Your lady has been doing a great job with him," said Karstetter. He knew when to change a subject.

"Gail's okay," grunted Bishop. "She's on the right wavelength. But we got to get her out too. Next time they won't miss."

"Carl."

Bishop looked up. "Yes?"

"You noticed one thing?"

"What?"

"Galov has never told us why he wants to come over. He's told her he wants to defect, but no reason. You check her reports."

"I have," said Bishop. "And that's exactly what impresses me."

"I don't see . . ."

"It's the strongest point in his favor," said Bishop. "What the hell do you want him to say? That he wants to defect because he likes apple pie, or that he's crazy about democracy? You can bet your bottom dollar that if he was a phony, he'd unload a whole ragbag of platitudes—how he can't stand communism, and wants to live in a free country so he can play baseball, that he believes in civil rights and Thanksgiving. No, Jack, I'm taken with a guy who just says, 'Hell, I want out. I've had enough of this sump.' "

"Hmm." Karstetter scraped butter on his toast. "Okay. But what is he selling us? Has he offered to bring us anything? Hand over some goodies? Pay his passage? What do we get out of it?"

Bishop had an irritating habit of assuming a tone of saintlike patience when he wanted to explain an operational matter to subordinates who, his manner would indicate, shouldn't need an explanation. He took that tone now as he said: "Our friend isn't a little clerk who we want to sneak a file out of a drawer, Jack. You know that. He's Special Service Section II. He's got it all in here." Bishop tapped his forehead. "He has the tab on the people they infiltrate—the TASS correspondents, the phony exchange students, the Aeroflot personnel they operate. I don't want some old code or cipher manual they'll change anyway the moment they know he's gone. I want what he carries in his head, what he knows. It's not a bunch of papers I want. It's his brain."

Karstetter yawned, and went red. "I'm sorry," he apologized hastily. "It's jet lag."

"Sure," said Bishop curtly. "You'd better have a nap before you fly back."

Inwardly, Karstetter groaned. He knew what was coming.

"You'll be through with us in two or three hours, when we've gone over the technical details," announced Bishop, checking his watch. "Then I want you on a plane straight back. I want you back in Germany tomorrow."

"Okay, Carl," said Karstetter wearily. So much for the good night's sleep he had promised himself. Or the shopping for his wife.

"You'll brief Gail. She'll be his escort officer for the lift. But you're in local control. It's got to go right, Jack. I don't want any screw-up. And listen, I don't want anybody to get hurt."

"Do the Germans know, or are we on our own?" asked Karstetter. His eyes prickled with tiredness.

"Strictly on your own. They don't know a damn thing. So you realize what a hell of a row there'll be if you ball it up."

The light flashed, and Bishop got up, went to his desk, and pressed the button that unlocked the door for privileged visitors. No one could get on that floor, along that corridor, and to his door unless they had the maximum clearance. The badges that admitted here were very special.

The electrically controlled, padded door swung open, and the Admiral entered.

Karstetter got to his feet.

"Well, gentlemen, no problems?" asked the Admiral.

"Not so far," said Bishop.

"Glad to see you, Mr. Karstetter," said the Admiral. "They speak highly of you. One of our best station heads, I hear."

"Thank you, sir," said Karstetter. He looked across at Bishop, but the gray man seemed to avoid his eye.

"So, you're all set for Pheasant?"

"Yes, Admiral."

"Good, good. No adverse weather reports?" It was the Admiral's little pet phrase for hostile activity from the other side.

"Nothing unexpected, as I told you. But we're watching it."

The Admiral turned to Karstetter.

"I guess you'll be going back soon, to supervise things on the spot, eh?"

"I'm leaving later today," said Karstetter.

"Excellent." He gave them a wave of the hand. "Keep me posted, and good luck." Then he was gone and the electric door swung closed behind him.

"You got to be a politician to sit at that desk," said Bishop.

It was a remark Karstetter appreciated.

"If it's any encouragement, Jack," Bishop said as an afterthought, "we're holding a good hand. Whatever we get out of our KGB friend, we'll have a hell of a good score. Think of the impact it'll have once we can announce that a Soviet vice consul who is also a senior KGB intelligence officer has defected to the United States. Why, Jack, that's worth a crate of candy bars in psychological warfare alone." Bishop came as near to chuckling as he would allow himself.

The last thing he told Karstetter at Dulles Airport was: "Tell Gail I'm thinking of her, we're all thinking of her. Wish her good luck." He gave a twisted smile. "She'll need it. But don't tell her that."

Across Karstetter's mind flashed the big plaque in the entrance hall of the big complex at Langley. It was a memorial tablet for the members of the agency who had been killed in action. The names of some were there in full, but there were others who were indicated just by a gold star. Even in death, their identities were secret.

But as he entered the jumbo, some inner voice kept reminding him that there was plenty of room left on the plaque for other stars. . . .

He shut his eyes as soon as he had fastened the seat belt. He was very tired.

Frankfurt

"I've had a letter from your mother," Shura announced unexpectedly.

He couldn't remember that happening before. His mother wrote periodically, and usually added a greeting

57

to Shura, but the letters were always addressed to him. The old lady was a creature of habit, and this wasn't like her.

"What on earth does she want?" Nicolai asked.

"She doesn't want anything," said Shura. "She sounds a little worried about you. She says she hopes you're not working too hard."

"I don't understand," he frowned. "Have you got the letter?"

"Here," said Shura.

It was really more of a short note, on just one page.

Darling Shura,

I hope you and Nicolai are well. He hasn't been keeping in touch very much, and it seems so long since I heard from him.

I know it is silly to worry, especially with you there to look after him, but you must forgive an old woman who sometimes imagines things. You must write to me frankly. Is everything all right? I know how dedicated my Nicolai is, but it is bad to work too hard all the time. Don't let him neglect you. If you have any worries, you must share your anxieties with me.

Is it not time that he had some leave, and you could both come home and have a few weeks' well-deserved holiday? I'm longing to see you, my darling Shura, and my wonderful son.

Write to me quickly and tell me all the news.

I embrace you.

Slowly he gave her back the letter.

"You've been neglecting her," said Shura accusingly. "When did you last write?"

"Oh, I don't know. A couple of weeks ago, I think." He was deliberately vague.

"You think, you think," said Shura. "She is your mother, Nicolai."

"I've never been the world's greatest letter-writer, you know that." He was trying to laugh it off. "Anyway, what is there to write about? 'Dear Mamushka, I go to the consulate, I go home, I sleep, I get up. I go to the consulate. . . .' "

"Is that all you do?" asked Shura quietly.

He swung around, the tie he was about to put on in front of the mirror in his hand.

"What is that supposed to mean?" he asked, not angrily. He was very much in control of himself.

"I suppose you were on duty when you stayed out all night. I suppose the woman I saw you with is just a colleague."

"Yes," he said blandly. "Absolutely correct. On both scores."

Her lips were trembling. "I don't believe you," she said.

He felt a terrible pang of guilt. He knew he was going to do something awful to her, and suddenly he wanted to explain everything, to take her into his confidence, to put every card in the deck on the table.

But he knew he did not dare.

"Shura," he said, "please. I . . . There are things I cannot explain. You will understand. One day. I hope you will."

She gave a little cry suddenly, and flung herself into his arms, her head on his shoulder, and sobbed.

"I love you, Nicolai," she cried. "I love you so much and I can't bear this . . . this wall between us. You've become so distant. Sometimes, I feel as if the man I married has disappeared and a stranger has taken his place."

"That's nonsense, babushka," he muttered. Gently he pushed her down into the chair by the dressing table.

"Everything is all right," he added, trying to be reassuring. "Honestly."

Her tear-stained face looked up at him "No, it isn't," she said, trying to control her sobs. "You're ruining your career. Do you know what they're thinking?" She stopped. She knew she had said too much.

"What are they thinking, my love?" he asked very calmly.

She was confused. She seemed to be searching for a way to shut the door she had opened. "They are concerned about you," she said at last. "Your . . . future."

"How do you know?" He was standing very still.

"Ivan Ivanovitch."

He gave a laugh. "Rostov! You mustn't take any notice of him!"

"Please, Nicolai," she pleaded, "he is your superior. He is a lieutenant-colonel in your service. *And* he likes you. So when he starts getting . . . anxious . . ."

"I didn't even know you'd seen Rostov," said Nicolai, a little sharply.

"Be reasonable. He is an old friend of my family. And that's another thing: why have you been so anxious to keep us apart. You never asked him here. You never took me to see him. You tried to make sure we didn't meet. Why? What were you afraid of?" Her tears had dried. Now she was the prosecutor.

"Afraid? You're fantasizing, Shura. You know I'm not a very social type." He was being defensive. "And you're right. He is senior in rank. He is my superior. It can be a little embarrassing, meeting socially. I see him every day on duty, so I feel a little awkward rubbing elbows with him after hours. You can understand, surely."

"You don't trust even me anymore," she said sadly.

He started to knot his tie. "That's very unfair," he said.

She jumped up, eyes blazing. "Damn you," she cried, "I'm not interested in being fair. You're my husband, the man I love, the man who is my life, and you're betraying me."

She rushed to the bedroom door and slammed it so that the walls shook.

Nicolai stared at himself in the mirror. He was white-faced.

Offenbach

They had arranged to meet, briefly, in Offenbach, four-teen kilometers from Frankfurt. The rendezvous was at the Leather Museum, with Gail due at 3 P.M. and Nicolai arriving ten minutes later.

He didn't drive from Frankfurt. Whenever he used his little Volkswagen, the black Mercedes dogged him. The mentality of the German security service amused Nicolai. It was very predictable. They followed his small car wherever he drove, waiting patiently outside the flat in the Wieserstrasse until he appeared, then cruising discreetly in the traffic after him. They stationed themselves across from the consulate and waited faithfully for him to get into his car again at day's end.

But if he went on foot, they left him alone. They just stayed parked, and the two men in front watched silently until he'd gone around the corner. Maybe they felt that unless he had wheels he was harmless. It was a logic he couldn't follow, but they methodically stuck to the pattern.

So Nicolai left the consulate on foot, walked around for a while, entered a department store by one entrance and exited by another, checked in shop windows a couple of times for any suspicious reflections, and finally strolled to the Bahnhof, where he hired a cab for Offenbach.

And couldn't get rid of the uneasy feeling that he hadn't fooled anybody.

When he finally paid off the cab, he reassured himself again. No, there wasn't anybody. No curious car, no loitering bystander.

Gail, as arranged, was already in the museum, seemingly engrossed in exhibits of embossed and gilded medieval leather work from Spain and Italy.

"Hello," he said, and she turned around and had, he thought, a look of relief when she saw him.

"No problems?" she asked.

"No."

It was only then she said: "Good to see you, Nick."

This part of the museum was empty, but they could hear the slow-paced tread of a man approaching from another room; doubtless a custodian on his eternal patrol.

"Is everything all right with you?" He hadn't seen her, after all, since the Sachsenhausen shooting.

She nodded. "Let's walk around," she suggested. They were keeping their voices low, as befit visitors to a museum.

"It's all set," she said.

"When?" he asked, and felt a tingle of excitement. "Where?"

"Very soon," she said. "Are you all ready?"

"I think so. From where?"

"I'll let you know."

He had a curious sense of anticlimax. Is this all there is to it? Just like that? Is this how a deserter felt when he bought the train ticket that took him away from his barracks?

"It could be dangerous, you know," she suddenly said. In a way, it sounded terribly naïve.

"So is crossing the street," he joked, trying to make light of it.

She halted in front of one of the glass cases. "No, Nick. You are taking a big risk."

"Gail," he said. "You shouldn't be talking like that. Not

61

to me. Your job is to convince me that it's the smartest thing that I've ever done. That everything is taken care of, that there's nothing to worry about."

"Of course, that's right. You don't need to worry." She bit her lip. "But you know a doctor always warns a patient about the risks an operation might entail—just as a precaution."

"Are you trying to talk me out of it?" he asked coldly.

The museum guard entered and slowly paced past them. He didn't even bother to give them a glance.

"Look," said Gail, for his benefit. "That's Napoleon's briefcase. Would you believe it?"

Nicolai peered at it. It looked worn, much used. "That must have had a few state secrets in it," he remarked, playing out the act.

The keeper disappeared into another room.

Nicolai's tone changed again. "What exactly are you trying to say?" he demanded.

"I'm only reminding you . . . of what you know anyway." The tip of her tongue flicked across her lip. Her lips were dry. "You're so important to . . . your people. They'll do everything to stop you. To kill you . . ."

"You're doing an excellent job trying to scare me out of it," he said, hard.

"No." She sounded a little frantic. "I want you to come over. As quickly as possible."

"So why—"

"Because I care for you." Her voice had risen a note. "Don't you understand? I want nothing to happen to you." She tried to hide her embarrassment.

"How unprofessional," said Nicolai. "You're really not a very good agent, I'm beginning to think. Did they train you that badly? I am surprised at you. What a disappointment."

She had collected herself. Now she was quite in control again. "You call me tomorrow. At this number." She gave him a piece of paper. "At 5 P.M." She snapped her handbag shut. "You're quite right, Nick. About the other. I was being stupid. I guess we're all under a strain. Forget it."

"I have already," he lied. "You leave now. I'll follow. And I'll call you tomorrow."

"I'll be waiting."

"By the way," he suddenly added, as if he had remembered something. "I haven't got any choice, you

know. Either way they'll be after me. You see, I suspect
that they suspect me."

She stared at him.

"So, dear Gail, whichever way I go, I don't think anybody will sell me life insurance." He tried to smile reassuringly. "There's no turning back now. For either of us."

He turned and left her standing. She heard his footsteps
echo in the other room.

Frankfurt

Shura had a diplomatic passport, so she passed through
immigration control at the airport without difficulty. But,
as a matter of routine, passport control immediately noti-
fied the duty officer from the security office. It was
standard procedure with Soviet official personnel.

She had a window seat in the British Airways plane,
and for the short flight across East German territory, she
read *Vogue*. It would be the last copy she'd see for some
time. Where she was going, the magazine was not available.

She only spent half an hour in Berlin, and then caught
the Aeroflot jet on which she was booked straight to
Moscow.

Washington

Bishop reread the decoded signal from the Bonn station.
It was routine, but he found it of special interest. It passed
on the information that the wife of the Soviet vice consul
in Frankfurt had gone to Moscow. Her husband apparently did not see her off at the airport.

He decided to send a special request to the Moscow
station asking them to keep an eye, if possible, on the do-
ings of Mrs. Nicolai Galov.

Already the Moscow people were trying to determine
at his bidding, if anything unusual was happening in
the life of Nicolai Galov's old mother. They had come up
with the useful information that she had apparently been
visited by an officer of KGB counterintelligence.

It really was high time, Bishop decided, that they got
Galov out of Frankfurt.

New York

All the bearded man in Central Park felt was a sudden sharp pain as the long needle entered his back. His nerves were paralyzed in a couple of seconds, and he slid off his canvas stool and fell against the easel with his half-painted picture.

Felix Thompson, who, as Feliks Tarasov, had defected from his post as KGB liaison officer in Warsaw in 1973, had been coming to the same spot at the same time for five days to work on his Central Park South cityscape. The regularity of his routine had become his death warrant.

The execution was done swiftly. The man in the steel-framed glasses had to time it perfectly, so that the traitor would die while no one was around. No easy thing in Central Park, but luckily it was a reasonably secluded spot.

The man had come up and watched Tarasov working, the way people do when an artist paints in public.

"I like it," he had even said.

The painter had not turned his head to look at him. "Thank you," he'd simply said, doing something to the roof of the Plaza Hotel with his paintbrush.

Then the needle had come out, and it was all over.

"Sorry," the killer said. He actually meant it. It was going to be a very nice painting, and the man in the glasses wouldn't have minded owning it.

If ever it would have been finished.

He was pleased he had decided to do the job here, rather than attempt it in Greenwich Village where Tarasov had gone underground, living the life of an artist in a studio his American hosts had provided for him. It would have been much trickier.

The man walked quickly from the scene, leaving Tarasov lying on the grass.

Near the Hotel Pierre, he hailed a yellow cab. "United Nations," he instructed the driver.

There, he showed his delegation pass to the guard. He was always punctilious about things like that.

64

Frankfurt

The moment Nicolai arrived at the consulate, he sensed the tension. Was it his imagination, or did the security man who opened the front door look slightly uneasy? Even Lenin, in his official framed portrait in the entrance hall, eyed him coldly, almost suspiciously.

He was waiting for the lift, to go down to the basement, when Nadia, the confidential secretary, appeared.

"Ah, the very man," she said. "Comrade Rostov wants to see you."

"Now?"

"He said as soon as you came in to report to him." Nadia liked him, and she could see he was puzzled. All this was out of the ordinary. The official summons via the secretary was itself unusual.

She walked with him, and suddenly he wondered if she were escorting him, to make sure he didn't wander off.

"General Modin is here," she half whispered.

He froze. "Modin?" he repeated dully.

She nodded.

Suddenly he knew he hadn't been imagining anything. It was trouble, big trouble.

Major General Vasili Modin. Head of the KGB Inspectorate. The man they all knew as The Auditor. When he appeared on the scene, it was the storm signal. They all feared the Inspectorate, the department that had the right to probe all of them, to check into everything they did. The men from the Inspectorate appeared when things were going wrong. And their boss was Modin, who had held the post under many Kremlin masters and never lost his power. Modin was the one man who made top KGB officials look over their shoulder.

"When did he arrive?" asked Nicolai in a whisper.

"Last night," said Nadia, also *sotto voce.* "Out of the blue."

So that was why Rostov wanted to see him urgently. To brief him about Modin's arrival. When the general was around, they were all allies against him. They had to make sure they all said the same thing.

They arrived at Rostov's door, and Nadia knocked.

"Enter," came Rostov's voice.

She stood aside, and Nicolai went in. His mouth was suddenly dry. The general was sitting in an armchair, eyes fixed on him as he entered. Rostov, looking tense, was behind his desk.

Nicolai's heart sank. He hadn't expected to come face to face with The Auditor so soon. He had fervently hoped to prepare himself for the ordeal. To get Rostov's briefing first and find out what it was all about.

"There you are, Captain Galov," said Rostov very formally, in the manner of a boss who had been kept waiting by an unpunctual subordinate. "The general has come from headquarters. It concerns you."

"Please sit down, Comrade Galov," said The Auditor. He was a massive man with a double chin. Like all of them, he wore a civilian suit. His graying hair was closely cropped. The surprising thing about him was his hands; they were sensitive, almost feminine hands, with long, slender fingers. They were so incongruous with his bulk that it was almost as if a mischievous quartermaster had issued him the wrong set.

It was not often that Modin came abroad. He did not involve himself in field operations. His concern was security and, above all, loyalty.

When he did travel, it was on a diplomatic passport that identified him as a representative of Amtorg, the Soviet state trading organization.

The Auditor reached over and took from Rostov's desk a small, black leather-bound book with a lock. The clasp was undone.

"This is your duty log?" asked Modin.

"Yes," said Nicolai. So it was what he had feared.

"And you have recorded all your movements in it, as required by regulations? Your daily activities? Every meeting with outsiders?"

"Yes, Comrade General. As required by regulations."

"How interesting," said Modin. "You appear to have been leading a very dull existence here, Galov."

Behind his desk, Rostov watched Nicolai.

"I was not aware that there was any dissatisfaction with my work," said Nicolai. He remembered the old chess maxim at the training school: "Sometimes your opponent may feel your position is not as weak as he believes it to be if you attack unexpectedly."

"Our directorate has had no complaint about the way

Comrade Galov has been carrying out his duties," added Rostov, greatly daring.

It was a mistake. Especially the reference to "our directorate."

"*Your* directorate!" sneered The Auditor. "You people forget we have nine directorates. You think yourself the elite, but to me you matter no more than any of them. We in the Inspectorate have our own views on the efficiency of some of your sections, believe me. There is no room for adventurism in our work, comrades. The ministry will not have it. I will not have it. You operate by the regulations, or I will see to it that you operate not at all, I promise you."

Nicolai had always avoided becoming involved in KGB politics. He knew there was an intense rivalry between the various covert branches, that departments sometimes spent as much time undermining each other as they did combating the enemy, He had known all along that it was wisest not to become embroiled in such machinations. And he suddenly realized that The Auditor was not just after him; he was going to seize this chance to cut the throats of as many people as he could; it was a golden opportunity to get at Special Service Section II, the crack division whose aloof status was a thorn in the Inspectorate's side.

"I think we understand each other, correct?" smiled The Auditor icily. He had gold teeth fillings, further proof of his exalted status in Soviet society.

"There has never been any question of it, General," Rostov hastily replied.

The Auditor nodded. He liked cowing his opponents. "Now then, Galov. Curious rumors about you have been reaching Moscow. Not the kind of rumors we should hear about a member of the KGB. Rumors that are so disturbing that I have had to come here to see things for myself."

He turned on Rostov.

"I have to say, Colonel, that it does not speak highly for the operation of this station that it has come to this."

"And what are these rumors precisely, Comrade General?" Nicolai demanded haughtily.

Modin inhaled a deep breath, reminiscent of a bull about to charge. But Nicolai gave him no chance.

"In fact," he went on, "am I being accused of something?"

Instead of the roar he expected, the general was remarkably restrained.

"Why should you be?" he asked. "Do you feel yourself guilty of something?"

From behind his desk, Rostov suddenly said: "You didn't tell me Shura had returned to Moscow."

"Is that against regulations, Comrade?" inquired Nicolai, still on the offensive. "Must one ask permission for one's wife to go on a little holiday?"

The Auditor was interested. "Oh, is that what she is having, Comrade? A little holiday?" He scowled. "You have made her very unhappy, Galov."

"And since when is the Inspectorate concerned about matrimonial relationships?"

This time Nicolai had made the mistake.

"Don't play the fool with me," growled Modin. "I do not come all this distance because for the moment you are not sleeping together. Your attitude, your behavior, your movements are sufficient to give us cause for alarm."

He turned to Rostov. "You explain to him, Colonel," he said impatiently. "You *are* his superior."

Rostov shifted uncomfortably. "Reports have reached the Inspectorate from . . . er, various sources suggesting dissatisfaction on your part, Nicolai," he said. "There have been unexplained absences from home. Your movements . . . you have not explained them. You have not been reporting all your contacts and meetings. You have avoided taking home leave. For a man in your position . . ."

He left the rest unsaid, but the general jumped in. "It is quite enough to warrant disciplinary action," he said sternly. "Don't delude yourself that because you are on special operations, such conduct can be overlooked. You are relieved of secret duties."

Nicolai stood up, slowly.

"You are not to handle or process any classified documents. Access to the Referentura is forbidden to you from now on."

"Am I under arrest?" asked Nicolai quietly.

"Shall we say that for the moment you are suspended. A further decision will be made by the appropriate authority," rasped the general. "Consider yourself restricted to your quarters, for the next twenty-four hours."

"And then?"

"You will be reassigned."

You mean, taken to Moscow under escort, thought Nicolai. Rostov's face, behind the desk, said as much.

"I would welcome the opportunity of clearing myself of any allegations," Nicolai declared, almost for the record.

"Good," nodded the general. "Good. You will be given every opportunity."

Nicolai pulled out the official keys and laid them on the desk.

"It is sad to see the son of a Hero of the Soviet Union under such a cloud," said Modin.

Outside, Rostov walked with Nicolai to the front door.

"I am sorry," he said. "It is out of my hands. You know the Inspectorate . . . the moment they get their claws on something . . ."

"Good-bye," said Nicolai.

The air in the Beethovenstrasse smelt good and he took a deep breath. He knew why he had been able to leave the building. They were curious what he would do next. If they were watching him, they were surprised to see him leave his Volkswagen where it was. By now, he figured, it might even have been surreptitiously fitted with a directional bug that would enable them to tag him. No point making life easier for anybody.

As usual, the black Mercedes was in its place, watching the building. As he started to stroll off, it made no move. The two men in plainclothes stared at him, quite openly, but stayed put.

He crossed the street and could not resist glancing at the roof of the consulate, at the big radio aerial that kept in touch, over the special channel, with the communications central deep in East Germany and headquarters in Moscow.

By now, reckoned Nicolai, there might be an urgent cipher message about him going out into the ether.

Fort Meade

He was right. The Army Security Agency monitoring station near Heidelberg picked it up, and within ten minutes it was relayed to NSA headquarters across the Atlantic.

There the computers began to whir and hum, and they quickly identified the cipher groupings. It was a new code, and they had nicknamed it Circus. They knew it was reserved for instant, ultrasecret communication, chiefly originating through diplomatic channels. It was only rarely transmitted, and they suspected it was reserved for KGB and GRU use.

The origin, Frankfurt, was of special interest, since an alert notice had just been issued from Washington that radio transmissions originating from the Soviet Consulate in Frankfurt were currently of extreme interest.

The Fort Meade duty officer called Bishop himself. "I thought you'd be interested to know that their Frankfurt station had just sent an urgent Circus message to Moscow," he reported.

"I thought they might," Bishop said, leaving the duty officer highly curious. "Any luck?"

"We're still trying to crack it, but you know what a son of a bitch Circus is," said the duty officer.

"Keep trying," ordered Bishop. "I have an idea what it might be about, but I want to make sure."

He left the duty officer a very puzzled man.

Frankfurt

Nicolai recognized the green Opel immediately. It was one of the consulate cars, and it was parked outside his small block of flats in the Wieserstrasse.

You don't waste time, General, Nicolai said to himself.

It was typical that they didn't care it was an official car, with its diplomatic plate. The gloves were off.

Nicolai looked up at his flat, but from this vantage there was nothing unusual to be seen.

Nobody was hanging about in the street, either.

Nicolai went around the corner, to the fire escape at the back of the building. There, too, it seemed all clear. Slowly he began to climb up the fire escape to his floor. There he took out the key to the back door, and unlocked it. He was in the kitchen.

Very quietly, he went into the corridor. The door of the living room stood open, and somebody was moving around behind it.

"Hello, Leonid," said Nicolai.

Leonid, the consulate's security man, swung around. He was in his shirtsleeves, his shoulder holster with the gun strapped to him. His jacket was neatly folded on the sofa.

The room was in disorder. Leonid had been ransacking it, pulling out drawers from the sideboard, ripping cushions, turning up the carpet, opening out books. He had a knife in his hand, and was just slashing the armchair to get at the stuffing.

He looked startled when he saw Nicolai. Startled and embarrassed.

"I . . . I'm sorry, Comrade," he said lamely. "Orders."

"Of course," said Nicolai amiably. "I expected it."

"Orders from the general," added Leonid, "you know how it is . . ."

"Indeed. Anything special you're looking for?"

"They said to see if there's anything . . . well, anything. Documents. Cameras. Film," said Leonid rather sheepishly.

"And have you found something?" asked Nicolai. He was smiling.

"Nothing," said Leonid, sounding relieved. "Not that I thought I would, Comrade. It is just a routine security check, I imagine."

He felt awkward. Nicolai was a KGB officer, a captain, a vice consul, a man whose authority had always been unquestioned, a man much superior to him in rank and status.

"Have you looked everywhere?" inquired Nicolai. "The bedroom? The bathroom? You must make sure, you know."

"That's all been done," said Leonid. "Everything is all clear."

"And now?" asked Nicolai. "What are your orders now?"

"Oh, now I just stay around with you. You can do what you like, go where you like, but I must be with you. Only for the time being." He put on his jacket. It was more proper. He was in the presence of a superior, after all. "I am sorry about the mess. When you don't know what you're looking for . . ."

"As long as they pay the landlord, I don't mind," said Nicolai.

Leonid was no longer nervous. He even began to feel grateful to Nicolai for the lack of fuss, the decent way he was taking it. He began to wonder if the Inspectorate wasn't making a hell of a mistake.

"Tell me, will you be with me all the time?" asked Nicolai.

"Yes, Comrade. But Sergei will relieve me at 1800 hours. He is doing the night shift."

Sergei was another of the security guards at the consulate.

"Well," said Nicolai lightly. "It must be a change from being cooped up in that basement."

"It can be very dull in the Referentura," Leonid agreed.

Nicolai nodded sympathetically. "Anyway, let's make ourselves comfortable. You'll be pleased to hear I have no plans to go anywhere. Try to tidy this place up as best you can, and I'll make us some tea."

"That would be nice, Comrade," said Leonid. How ridiculous to think this man was a security suspect.

The kitchen had hardly been touched in the search. Leonid obviously reckoned that if anything incriminating was hidden, it would be in the other parts of the flat. Toothpaste tubes, shaving-cream cannisters, and pillows were much higher on the list of hiding places than a tea kettle, one was taught at training school.

In the kitchen, Nicolai plugged in the electric kettle. "Would you like a piece of chocolate cake?" he called through the open door.

From the living room came Leonid's voice: "That would be very nice, Comrade Captain."

They were fast becoming friends.

Nicolai bent down and opened the door of one of the kitchen cupboards. He found the cardboard box with the shoe cleaning things. He took out the tins of black and brown shoe polish, the rags, a couple of brushes. At the bottom of the cardboard box lay the 9-mm Makarov pistol.

He had the pistol in his hand when he stepped softly into the living room. Leonid had put back some of the drawers, straightened one of the chairs that had fallen over, and was bent over the sofa, trying to put the ripped cushions straight.

Nicolai hit him on the back of the head with the butt of the pistol. The man had not even been aware that

Nicolai had come into the room, and he keeled over without a sound.

It had been a hard blow, delivered with Nicolai's full force, and it had fractured Leonid's skull. But as he lay unconscious, he merely looked asleep. A thin trickle of blood would emerge from his ear later.

Nicolai sighed. He had never disliked this dumb son of an ox.

But he had to move fast. He went into the bedroom, which was also in a state of disorder.

He grabbed a suitcase from the top of the wardrobe and hastily put some shirts, underclothes, and an alarm clock in it. He rushed to the bathroom for his toilet things, and put them into the case. He had to get away from this place as quickly as possible. He had to lose them.

Leonid must have the keys of the green Opel, but Nicolai decided against taking the car. With its special license plate, he might as well telegraph his whereabouts.

He took one more look around the bedroom. Yes, he had forgotten something. It was standing on the table beside the double bed. Shura's picture, in a silver frame.

Holding the photograph in his hand, Nicolai looked at her face. and his eyes were sad. Slowly he raised it to his lips and kissed the cold glass covering her face. Then he packed the picture and closed the suitcase.

He went into the living room and bent over Leonid. The man's face was pale. Nicolai felt his pulse. It was very weak. Nicolai bit his lips; he thought of getting help, an ambulance, anything. But it was now too risky.

A few moments later he emerged into Wieserstrasse, carrying the suitcase. The Opel was invitingly empty, but he ignored it.

He walked along several streets and then, suddenly, he hailed a cab. It was soon lost in traffic.

Frankfurt

"Everything is in order," said Rostov, shutting the safe. Behind the locked steel door of the Referentura, he had checked the secret files while Modin sat on one of the chairs, watching him silently.

Rostov had been thorough. He had gone through the

classified documents register, and then made sure each item was in place.

"Nothing is missing," added Rostov, to underline the point.

"He must be found," said Modin grimly. "As quickly as possible."

"Yes, General."

"Don't keep saying 'Yes, General,'" snapped Modin. "What are you doing about it?"

"We're looking for him." Rostov spoke without enthusiasm.

"How enterprising," said Modin sarcastically. "And where are you looking?"

Rostov kept cool. "All over, General."

"Discreetly, I hope?"

"Of course."

"If we do have to bring in the German police, we will say he is suffering from loss of memory," said Modin. "But avoid it if you can. Concentrate on our resources."

"It is being done."

"And what have you told the hospital? How did you explain it?"

"Our story is that Leonid hit his head while falling downstairs."

"And you think they believe it? One look at him and the doctor knows." Modin shook his head. "The ambulance should never have been called. He should have been brought here."

Rostov loathed this man. "General, he is critical. The base of his skull is fractured. He needs medical care. He would have died here. We have no such resources, as you know. This is not an embassy, with its own doctor. Immediate hospitalization was the only way to save his life . . . if it can be saved."

Modin waved one of his effeminate hands. "I too care for human life," he said airily, and then his tone became hard, "but there may have to be explanations. Especially if he dies in a German hospital. Far better to have him die here. We could have shipped the body out as diplomatic baggage and they would have been none the wiser." He rose. "The minister will not be pleased. You do not come out of this very well, Comrade Colonel."

"If that is your opinion, General," said Rostov stiffly.

He feared The Auditor, as the whole service did, but he too had some friends in the Kremlin.

"The whole business proves that your section and your directorate think you are a law unto yourself. I will recommend a total reorganization. Your activities need much closer supervision." Modin picked at one of his gold-filled teeth with his little finger. Something was stuck there and it annoyed him. "You were sent here to oversee special operations, I believe. I have no idea what, because your section likes to keep its secrets. But I tell you this, it hasn't worked out, Colonel, has it? Instead, you haven't even smelled out a traitor right under your nose."

"If any explanations are required from me, I will make them to the appropriate organs," said Rostov. It was a defiant declaration of war on the Inspectorate, and on its head.

"I see," said Modin softly. "Very well. The future will take care of that. Meanwhile, I want your man. I want Galov right here."

"And what happens then?"

"That, Ivan Ivanovitch, you will leave to me."

Rostov's lips tightened. He suddenly hoped that Nicolai would be dead before that ever happened. For his own sake.

Frankfurt

Gail stood by the phone booth. Her watch said 4:58.

Two minutes to go . . . If all were well, she knew he'd call on time. She had given him the number of this phone booth, and she also knew that he'd call her from one. Two phone booths talking to each other. It made their conversation secure.

A few seconds before five, she entered the booth. Almost immediately the bell shrilled. She picked up the receiver.

"Nick?" she said.

"Yes."

She felt a curious thrill of excitement at hearing his voice. She had not seen him for twenty-four hours, but he had been in her mind all her waking hours. And she hadn't had much sleep.

"Everything all right?" she asked.

"I think so."

"You sure?" There had been a hesitation before he had replied.

"I'm on the run," he said matter-of-factly.

Instinctively, she looked out of the phone booth. But there wasn't anybody hanging around.

"Where are you?"

"I'm all right. For the moment. But we've got to do it quickly."

"What happened?"

"They know," he said simply. "And I don't want them to find me. I'm sure you understand."

"All right. Tomorrow," she said. "Take the coach that leaves the Bahnhof for Rudesheim at 3 P.M. When you get there, go to the Lorelei, in the Drosselgasse. Got that? Be at the Lorelei at 4:15 exactly. I'll be there."

"Lorelei. 4:15 P.M. And then?"

"That's all you have to do," she said. There was a pause. "Are you safe till then?"

"I hope so," he said. "I've got a room. They call it a hotel. Nobody will find me there. Not in that place."

"It sounds like a whorehouse," she said, but even her slight laugh was tense.

"I should be safe. Till tomorrow."

"You'll be on your own, of course," she said. "It was a good idea sending your wife to Moscow."

"Gail . . ." he began, but she interrupted him.

"We'll have lots of time to talk soon, Nick. Not now. Three P.M. coach to Rudesheim. The Lorelei at 4:15 P.M. On the dot."

"Can't you do it sooner. Tomorrow is a long way off."

"No," she said firmly.

"Okay," he said dully.

"And take care of yourself, Nick." Her voice was very soft. Then she put the phone down.

Nicolai came out of his phone booth. Something troubled him. Maybe it was her remark about Shura being in Moscow. He had never told her . . .

But he had to go through with it, anyway. It was too late now to pull back. Much too late.

He tried to reason out why they were waiting twenty-four hours to lift him. After all, he had told her that he was on the run, that they were after him.

Then he knew why. They wanted to see if his pals

were really hunting him. They wanted to see how far they'd go. How anxious they were to get hold of him.

He wondered suddenly if even Gail trusted him.

And if he could trust her.

Washington

When his section had an operational mission underway in the field, Bishop always remained overnight in his office. It became his self-enclosed world; he slept on a camp bed, he kept an electric coffeemaker on the boil all night, he had a change of clothes available in the closet, and he never strayed far from his battery of communications—telephones, secure direct lines, intercoms, links with the operation center at Langley, and the round-the-clock ears of the agency at Fort Meade.

At such times, he would sit in his armchair in the middle of the night, and study the operation's key file, going over every detail once again, reassessing every fact. Sometimes the picture became clearer, and he felt reassured that everything had been taken care of. But occasionally, he would read and reread a page, analyzing some fact that had not seemed so important earlier. Sometimes a danger signal would start to glow, and he would not lie on the camp bed at all. He'd remain slumped in the chair, trying to resolve these last-minute doubts that might have come too late.

The Pheasant dossier made interesting reading. Especially the reports from Gail. Karstetter's comments were more detached, cautious, objective, as befitted the chief of station and the supervisor of the field agent.

Bishop poured himself his fourth cup of coffee in an hour. The train was rolling. Countdown had begun. He closed his eyes wearily as he sat back with the coffee at his elbow and tried to visualize the actors in the play he was masterminding. Gail, cool, beautiful, restless, a woman trying to fulfill herself through her secret-agent role. Karstetter, shrewd, harassed, weighed down with family responsibilities, but experienced, dedicated, a veteran of key agency operations.

And Nicolai. They had never met, but Bishop felt he

knew him. His thick file of photos made Galov as familiar a face as those of his colleagues down the corridor. And yet . . .

Nicolai Galov remained the enigma.

Once he had him in his hands, Bishop promised himself that he was going to unpeel Galov like an onion. Layer by layer.

Lying on the coffee table next to him was a much thinner file. It contained only one sheet of paper with four names written on it:

Bogdan Karlovski. Rudolf Gabrilovich. Fedor Kravisky. Feliks Tarasov.

Four dead defectors.

Bishop always kept the sheet of paper at hand, to remind himself constantly that four defectors who were his charges had become targets.

The question was, who was the next one?

Frankfurt

Nicolai slowly tore up the airline ticket to Zurich. The plane was leaving in two hours, but he wouldn't be on it.

He had booked the flight as part of the false trail he had been laying. There was the hotel reservation he had made at the Intercontinental, and the one at the Atlantic. A rented car had been reserved. All in his name. Nicolai Galov. Quite openly, even showing his passport where needed, making no secret of the fact that he was a Soviet citizen, and a diplomat at that. It should leak out.

He hoped it would mislead Modin's hounds. More than likely they would pick up one of the trails and waste their time pursuing it. It might give him some breathing space.

In an hour, he was due to catch the Rudesheim bus. In two hours, he was due at the rendezvous . . . and Gail. Gail, who had been in his thoughts so much. He found her exciting and desirable, and now it would not be long before he could tell her the things he had been wanting to say.

Unless they caught up with him. Unless, in the next two hours, he was going to be dead.

The little hotel he had picked as a hideout was shabby

and out of the way. It was found in no tourist guide, and its down-at-the-heels exterior would attract only those who wanted anonymity or were broke.

He had paid in advance, and the blowzy woman behind the reception desk hadn't cared a damn after that. The name he gave was false, but they never cared anyway. As long as he paid, he could do what he liked behind his door, sleep with whomever he wanted. Moselstrasse tarts, GI deserters, petty crooks on the run, men who wanted to lie low, as he did, these were the clients of the Hotel Elsa in the Gutterstrasse. It was a good place to go underground.

Nicolai slept fitfully on the uncomfortable, creaking bed, and in the morning his eyelids were leaden. But at last the hour was coming. . . .

Suddenly he stiffened. He was sure he heard the floorboards creak outside his door. He stood rock still, and heard the sound of somebody breathing heavily. The door, its paint peeling, was dreadfully thin, and every time a person walked down the corridor, he heard their footsteps on the threadbare carpet covering the rotted wooden floorboards.

But this sound was different. Somebody was lurking outside his door. There was a scratching, like somebody trying to pick the lock. Nicolai reached for the knob and flung the door open. He had a glimpse of a figure crouching against it, then losing its balance as he tore it open.

It was a man who gave a gasp as he fell forward into the room just as Nicolai hit him on the jaw. The man rolled over on the floor and lay still.

Nicolai glanced up and down the corridor. It was empty. He shut the door, and then knelt down alongside the man. Only then did Nicolai see that the man had dropped a spring knife, with a long, thin, sharp blade.

The man was out cold. His face, sallow, ratlike, meant nothing to Nicolai. Certainly he wasn't one of the consular people. Nicolai reached into his inside pockets, but all he found was a worn billfold, with a ten-DM note in it, a railway ticket to Darmstadt, and a driver's license, issued in Essen, in the name of Hoffman. There was also a dirty handkerchief, a comb, and a stick of chewing gum.

Well, Herr Hoffman, Nicolai thought to himself, you're not one of my lot, that's for sure. You just don't fit the firm. But you were lurking outside my room, about to break in, and you did have your nasty little knife out. So who the hell are you? Were you paid for this job, or are you simply a sneak thief who goes for easy pickings in a fleabag like the Hotel Elsa?

One thing was sure. It was high time to get out.

Nicolai did nothing about the intruder. He was still unconscious, and by the time he woke up, Nicolai would be long gone.

His suitcase he left on the bed. It had become useless ballast. But Shura's photograph he took out of the silver ornamental frame. He put it in his wallet. The frame he tossed aside; it was too bulky.

"Auf wiedersehen, Kamerad," Nicolai said to the man on the floor.

Nicolai went down the rickety stairs, then walked out of the Hotel Elsa without saying a word to the receptionist. The blowzy woman had been replaced by an unshaven Turk, who didn't even look up as Nicolai passed. The room was paid up for three days, and until then he could do as he liked. In passing, Nicolai wondered if Herr Hoffman, when he woke up, would sneak out as he was doing, or make a fuss about being knocked out by the missing occupant of room 5.

Outside, in the fresh air, Nicolai took a deep breath. It made him aware how foul the air had been in the hotel. All night he had been breathing nothing but stale, cabbage-scented air. Hoffman must have been very hard up to pick on a dump like that for his hotel thieving.

He was out of cigarettes, so the first thing he did was to find a tobacconist.

"Amerikaner?" asked the girl in the kiosk.

It surprised Nicolai. He had never considered that he spoke German with an American accent. He just shook his head and smiled. Outside, he stopped to light a cigarette, which gave him a chance to spy out if he was under surveillance. He stared into several shop windows, studying not the goods on display but the reflections in the glass. They were reassuring.

Slowly he strolled toward the Bahnhof area. He didn't want to arrive too early and have to hang around the bus stop. He walked along the Kaiserstrasse, wondering if Hoffman had woken up yet.

The milling crowds around him, the stream of autos in the roadway, the policemen on traffic duty, even the noise—all strengthened his feeling of confidence. Not that he wasn't well aware of the fact that crowded places wouldn't stop his colleagues if they caught up with him. Hadn't he himself received special training on how to carry out a "wet affair" in a public place?

He had the Makarov in his pocket, and the grip of the pistol made him more secure still. He wasn't going to be an unsuspecting target if he could help it.

When he finally got to the bus stop, the coach was already in and people were boarding it. He had timed it perfectly. Then, as he was about to get into the coach, he saw the black Mercedes.

Or, at the very least, *a* black Mercedes.

He couldn't see who was in it, and his sudden panic subsided as his self-control took over. After all, Frankfurt was full of black Mercedes. And as far as he knew, the one that dogged him belonged to German security. Bonn's counterintelligence was hardly likely to stop his defecting. But if it were them, they had abandoned their usual routine of only following him when he was in a car.

If it were them at all . . .

He boarded the coach and found a window seat. He settled back, realizing his shirt was sticking to him. Another car had pulled up alongside the Mercedes, masking it. Well, if he couldn't see it, its occupants couldn't see him either. He relaxed.

He bought his ticket and slumped in his seat. He wanted to close his eyes and doze. It would be marvelous, he thought, to wake up and find himself already in Rudesheim; but he knew he was too tense for that to happen.

Just as the coach was about to start, a woman came running for it. She was portly and it was an effort; she waved an umbrella, signaling the driver not to leave. Puffing, she managed to get on board smiling apologetically to him. And behind her was Eddie Haze.

The woman, in her sensible tweeds and brogues, pushed her way along the center of the bus. She spotted the empty seat next to Nicolai, and plunked herself down beside him.

"*Hab's gemacht, nicht war?*" she said to Nicolai smugly.

Haze didn't appear to see Nicolai. He passed along the aisle, clutching a newspaper and sat down right at

81

the back, by the rear window. As the bus started, Nicolai twisted his head to look at him.

Haze was already engrossed in his paper. He appeared to be doing the crossword, and didn't even glance up as the bus started.

For some reason he couldn't quite make out, the bus, as it pulled away, had become dangerous to Nicolai. He suddenly felt as if death were a fellow passenger.

Autobahn

Nicolai was no longer tired. He watched the suburbs of Frankfurt flash by, and then they were on the autobahn, going south.

The back of his neck prickled. It felt as if Haze's eyes were boring into him, but when he sneaked another quick, surreptitious look, Haze was still busy with his crossword.

The tweedy woman dove into her voluminous bag and brought out a packet of sandwiches. Thick pieces of sausage peeped out from between the slices of pumpernickel. She took a big bite, and her jaws chomped up and down noisily as she masticated her snack.

How German, thought Nicolai, with dislike. He had never liked these people, not just because he was Russian and they had tried to destroy his homeland, killing his father in the process. They could be so gross, like this creature beside him.

He looked out the window. He wondered if the bus was being followed, but there were many cars on the autobahn, and he couldn't see behind the bus.

He tried to reason with himself. What did it matter that Haze was on the bus? He was with the Americans, after all. He had done exactly the service Nicolai had wanted him to; made the first contact. There could be no danger from him. Perhaps it was just coincidence that he was on the same coach. Why shouldn't he make a trip to Rudesheim? Or maybe he was there precisely because Nicolai was on it. Gail's people might well have asked him to keep a friendly eye on things until he arrived at the rendezvous.

Nicolai studied the other passengers. A priest, reading a black-bound book, his lips moving silently. Three students, complete with rucksacks. Traveling by bus was, after all, the cheap way. The backs and heads in front of him all seemed perfectly ordinary, unfamiliar and anonymous. A couple of businessmen, maybe, a few tourists. No need to feel uneasy, Nicolai, he kept telling himself.

He was not a nervous person. They had realized when they first recruited him that he was cool, even-tempered, full of common sense. It was as unusual for him to be anxious like this as it was for an athlete suddenly to have a high temperature.

According to his watch, it wouldn't be long now. Straight off the bus, down to the Drosselgasse—and Gail. He tried to figure out what they'd do with him. Straight to a U.S. Army camp? Or their headquarters in Heidelberg? Or into some hideout? Maybe their station in Munich?

He knew how his people would handle it. It would be interesting to see how the Americans did it.

The tweedy woman was snoring. Having consumed her snack, she lay back in the seat, nose shiny, mouth open, an unlovely sight.

He tried to shut her out. Now that he was about to take the final step, he thought again about his mother. The less she knew the better. He knew the shock would be terrible, and yet he hoped they would do it all very gently. She was not part of any of it. Even the Inspectorate must know that. So the old lady should be all right. And Shura . . .

Poor Shura. Caught up in something she didn't understand. They would tell her about Gail, he knew that, and make that the reason for what had happened. Shura, who would believe it was all for the sake of another woman and end up bitter, and very hurt.

Yes, poor Shura.

The two women in Moscow, one so proud and old, the other so beautiful and frustrated. Both were so much in his thoughts, making the thing he was doing so difficult.

Perhaps one day they would be able to forgive him. Perhaps . . .

The bus had swung off the autobahn, and was now driving alongside spreading vineyards. They were nearly there.

The woman gave a final rasping snore, and woke up. She gave him a stupid smile.

"Wir sind bald dar, nicht war?" she said, and he nodded. She started stuffing greaseproof paper, the remnants of her sandwich wrapping, back into her bag.

Then the bus slowed down, made a final turn, and slid to a halt.

"Rudesheim," shouted the driver, and all over the coach people started collecting their things and getting to their feet.

Nicolai gripped the pistol in his pocket. Slowly he stood up.

It was fifteen minutes to the deadline.

Rudesheim

There were people everywhere. It was as crowded as market day in a village. Nicolai got off the bus and tried to get his bearings.

"Well, what do you know?" said a voice behind him. "It *is* you."

Haze was at his side, the folded newspaper under his arm.

"I thought I saw you on the bus, but I wasn't sure. Don't tell me you've come for the fest."

What the hell is he playing at? Nicolai wondered.

But Haze was still in full stride. "Didn't know you fellows were interested in this kind of thing," he said.

The minutes were ticking on. Nicolai was anxious to get away.

"I have to get on," said Nicolai. "Excuse me."

"The place to be is the Drosselgasse, that's where it all happens," said Haze.

"Really?" Nicolai was wary.

"Come on, let's go there," said Haze. "Might as well do the wine festival together, eh?"

The wine festival! That explained the crowds all around. Nicolai had thought of Rudesheim as a sleepy little town on the banks of the Rhine, not this whirlpool of people jostling and pushing each other.

They started through the ever-thickening crush.

"Hey, look at this," said Haze. They came to a corner stall where an old man was selling bottles of wine. "Dirt cheap. A real steal. Let's get ourselves a couple. Might as well start the way we mean to end, eh?"

"I'm sorry," said Nicolai. "I'm in a hurry."

"You sound like a fellow who's got a date," Haze smiled, conspiratorially. "Where are you meeting her?"

"How do you know it's a her?" Nicolai asked sharply.

Haze nudged him in the ribs. "An educated guess. And I bet it's in the Drosselgasse."

"Why the Drosselgasse?" He was becoming more anxious by the moment.

"In Rudesheim, there is only the Drosselgasse," Haze replied disarmingly.

Colored lights were strung between the old houses. It wasn't dark yet, but it was easy to imagine how attractive they would look once they were lit.

As they neared the center of town, progress was still slower. Nicolai became increasingly tense. A mob like this could be used as a trap. Somebody could slip a knife into him with no one the wiser. He looked around for Haze. The man had fallen behind.

"Hey," he heard him shout across the crowd, "if we lose each other, I'll catch up with you."

Then Haze disappeared in the sea of faces. Nicolai pushed forward. Time was running short.

In the distance, out of sight, a brass band was playing oom-pah-pah music. People were singing.

Then he was pushed in the ribs, violently. It hurt. Somebody had shoved an elbow into him. But he could hardly turn, the crush was so great.

It was outside a house with green garlands on a striped pole that he caught a glimpse of a face he knew. Berezin. Berezin, who in Vienna had been Department V's technician. Specialist. Killer. The expert in *mokrie dela*. Wet affairs. The spilling of blood.

Nicolai knew they were closing in on him.

Across the revelers who separated them, Berezin and Nicolai stared at each other. Berezin was unsmiling—and trying to push toward him.

Nicolai was only yards from the Drosselgasse. The long alley, leading down to the Rhine, was a mass of faces, a human barricade blocking him. Hundreds of people milled around the inns that lined both sides of the gasse. People were singing, even trying to dance drunkenly.

Nicolai glanced back. Berezin was trying to push forward to get to him.

The throng behind him was edging Nicolai forward.

Everybody wanted to get down the Drosselgasse. The impetus was like a tide sweeping him on. He kept his hand on his pistol. He knew that was what Berezin was doing too.

Absurdly it flashed through his mind that Berezin probably had a Stetchkin, fitted with a silencer. It had been his favorite weapon in Vienna.

Over the heads of the crowd, he could see the gothic letters of the inn: DIE LORELEI. He glanced at his watch. He was already five minutes late.

Nicolai moved forward, furiously elbowing, shoving, pushing. He had to get there as quickly as possible, all the while keeping the crowd between him and Berezin.

He had no time to sort things out in his mind. They knew he'd be coming here, that was clear. They had not only picked up his trail they had been waiting. He was sure of that. And The Auditor hadn't relied on the local detachment; he was sure that Modin had brought Berezin with him. The Inspectorate liked to use its own people.

A girl threw her arms around Nicolai and kissed his cheek, spilling wine from the glass she was holding all over him. He thrust her aside. The Lorelei was close. So close.

He glanced backward. He couldn't see Berezin in the mob, but he knew he was still there, clawing his way nearer.

The front of the Lorelei was jammed with drinkers, sitting at tables, on the ground, on the steps of the inn. Desperately he tried to spot her. She must be anxious by now. She must be wondering what had happened to him.

But there was no sign of Gail.

Nicolai stumbled over a drunk, pushed past people, panting, his mouth dry, trying to make his way into the inn.

An arm grabbed him.

"You're late, Mr. Galov," said a man in a brown suit. He spoke in English.

He started propelling Nicolai into the inn.

"My name is Karstetter," said the man. "Let's get out of this."

Suddenly he stopped. An expression of astonishment crossed his face.

"Get inside," he gasped, and then he staggered forward and Nicolai saw the red stain spreading from the little hole in his back.

He never heard the shot. As always, Berezin used a silencer.

And he never wasted his bullets.

Karstetter looked like just another drunk, as he lay sprawled, his eyes glazed. There was one difference. He was dead.

Rudesheim

He stood aghast, looking at the body of Karstetter.

Then Gail was at his side, white-faced. Incongruously, that ridiculous camera was slung around her neck. She wore a sweater and slacks, he remembered that later, and she was pushing him into the inn.

"He's dead," said Nicolai foolishly, as if he expected her to do something about it. But she shook her head.

"Quickly," she said, pulling him into the inn. "Get out of sight."

It was smoky inside, and very noisy. The place was packed and the crowd was cheering a couple who were dancing on the bar counter.

"Follow me," said Gail. She had taken the lead and, like an expert navigator, she was steering him through the crowd.

They came out in the beer garden at the back. People were sitting at tables and a trio in lederhosen were playing, two accordionists and a violinist, he recalled later.

There was a gate in the garden wall, which Gail opened. She pushed the gate with the sureness of somebody who knew in advance that it wouldn't be locked.

"This way," she commanded tersely.

Now they were in a small back street where it was amazingly quiet after the hubbub they'd just left. Gail started running down it and he followed her.

They turned the corner and ran down some stone steps. At the bottom, Gail turned. They were both short of breath.

"Are you all right?" she asked anxiously.

He nodded.

"Come on then."

They were now walking parallel with the river, past some souvenir stalls. There were more people about now, but the crowds were thinner than in the center of town.

"Wait," said Nicolai.

She frowned as he stopped. "There's no time, dammit," she cried.

"I want a good look," Nicolai snapped grimly.

He glanced back at the way they had just come. Berezin wasn't in sight.

She read his thoughts. "No, I think we've lost them. For now."

She started half-walking, half-running, and he kept up with her.

"Them"? Why had she said "them"? Were there more than Berezin? And how did she know?

"Thank God," Gail said suddenly. She had spotted the black station wagon, parked by a boathouse. Its motor was running and a black man in a windbreaker sat behind the wheel. He had been looking out for them. He leaned over and unlocked the passenger door at the back.

"Get in," Gail almost shouted. She scrambled into the station wagon and Nicolai followed. He slammed the door as the car shot forward with such a jerk that Nicolai nearly hit his head.

They were going at high speed, with the driver sounding his horn savagely as some unsuspecting reveler got in his way.

Gail was lighting a cigarette. Her hand shook a little. "You want one?"

He took it and she lit his, too.

The black man looked military, thought Nicolai, despite his civilian getup.

Gail saw Nicolai stare at her, but said nothing.

"What about your man? Back there?" said Nicolai. "You just left him lying . . ."

Gail blew out some smoke. "That's not our problem," she said. "Not now—getting you away safely, that's what matters."

He had never realized she could be so cold-blooded. And yet he grudgingly admired her. Once he had accused her of being unprofessional. There was nothing unprofessional about her now. She could be one of his own people when she was like this.

"What next?" asked Nicolai.

"You'll see," she said.

He felt angry. He wanted to say: Hell, it's my neck too. I'm entitled to know what's happening, where you're taking me.

"How the hell did they know, Nick?" she said suddenly.

He shrugged. "Maybe I ought to ask you."

"What's that supposed to mean?" she demanded icily.

He stubbed out his cigarette in the ashtray. His mouth was too dry to smoke.

"Well," he said, "I didn't tell them, that's for sure."

They were on the autobahn now, tearing along in the direction of Frankfurt. He recognized an asparagus field he had passed in the bus.

The black driver picked up a radio telephone at his side.

"Pheasant," he said. "Are you receiving?"

There was a crackle of static, and then an American voice said: "Loud and clear. Go ahead, Pheasant."

"Pheasant caught," said the driver.

"Roger," said the voice.

"Out." The driver put his phone back.

"Who's Pheasant?" asked Nicolai.

"You," said Gail, and for the first time she allowed herself a hint of a smile.

"And I've been caught?"

"It's only a way of speaking, Nick," she said reassuringly. "You know radio messages."

She leaned forward to the driver.

"What's our ETA, Jesse?" she asked.

"Half an hour. If all goes well."

She sat back with a sigh.

"Well, at least you're in one piece, Nick," she said softly. He was suddenly aware of her nearness.

He wished she didn't have slacks on. He liked her legs. He said: "I'm sorry things went wrong."

She nodded. "Tell me, what happened?" she asked, changing the subject. "Why did you go on the run? What tipped them off?"

"Later," said Nicolai. He took her hand. It was cold.

"Listen, Gail . . ." he began, and stopped. He could see Jesse's eyes in the rearview mirror, studying them.

"Yes?" She hadn't pushed his hand away.

"Nothing. It's just that . . . well, I'm glad you're here."

She gave his hand a squeeze, and then withdrew hers. But she said softly: "So am I."

The station wagon accelerated. Nicolai saw the speedometer needle climb to 90 . . . 95 . . .

"Shit," said Jesse. Then he stared into his driving mirror. He reached for the radio phone again.

"Pheasant," he said, "do you read me?"

"Go ahead, Pheasant," said the voice.

"They're on to us," said Jesse.

The radio voice sounded more urgent. "How many?"

"One car. Following us."

Nicolai craned his neck to look out of the back window. A gray car was about half a mile behind them.

"Okay, Pheasant, keep going. I'll get backup onto it."

"Roger," Jesse said, and put his foot down even harder.

Gail looked worried. "What's our backup?" she asked.

"Don't worry about it," said Jesse. "Better worry about them. They've been on our tail for the last ten miles."

"Can't you shake them off?"

"On an autobahn? You must be kidding."

He was now doing 100, his eyes flicking to the driving mirror every few moments.

"As long as we can stay ahead, we'll be okay," he volunteered. "I think."

They heard the helicopter overhead, and then it swooped lower, and hovered over the gray car. The chopper had olive-drab paint and U.S. Army markings.

The gray car slowed up a little.

Jesse chuckled.

"I guess they won't do nothing mean with that bird on top of them."

They came level with a green-and-white police car parked on the hard shoulder of the autobahn. Despite their high speed, it ignored them. But then it pulled out, its blue light revolving, and as the gray car neared, it drew level with it. A policeman's arm started waving it down. Gradually, reluctantly, the gray car pulled up by the side of the speedway.

"You have influence," said Nicolai. "Some backup. Army. Police."

"Don't sound so impressed," Jesse grinned. "It'll make 'em big-headed."

"Ten minutes," said Gail. "In ten minutes, it'll be all over, Nick."

And suddenly the three of them were silent.

Washington

The decoding machine chattered out the flash signal and within three minutes it was on Bishop's desk.

He ripped open the "Eyes Only" envelope and swore under his breath. Then he picked up the direct line to the Admiral.

"Bad news," he said. "It's Pheasant. Our station chief's been killed."

There was a pause.

Then the Admiral asked: "What happened?"

"I've got no details yet. There must have been a shootout at the pickup. I'll let you know the moment anything comes in."

"What about Pheasant himself? Have we got him?"

"Yes. He's been lifted."

"At least we got him. Er . . . Carl . . ."

"Yes, sir?"

"Karstetter's family," said the Admiral. "Have they been told?"

"I guess the embassy in Bonn will do that," Bishop said irritably. He had other things on his mind.

Rhine-Main

The terraced vineyards and the Rhine had been left miles behind, and now they were driving past fir trees and a tall wire fence. Jesse swung the station wagon along a road through a wood, and suddenly they came to a blue notice board that announced that they had reached Rhine-Main Air Force Base.

A white-capped armed air policeman waved them to a halt, but as soon as he saw the ID card Jesse flashed at him he let them through. As if by prearrangement, a jeep swung out in front of them, and they followed it into the air base.

Nicolai didn't conceal his interest as the station wagon followed the jeep through the installation, past barracks and hangars, and Air Force aircraft scattered along the runways. Hercules transports towered above the smaller planes. One had just landed, and a long, thin line of infantrymen was emerging from it.

Two civilians stood by a radar trailer and Jesse, who seemed to know exactly what to do, pulled up alongside them. They both got into the station wagon, one beside Jesse and the other in the back, next to Nicolai.

They looked like identical twins, thought Nicolai. The same short haircuts, the same tan raincoats, identical button-down shirts, and almost identical ties.

The man next to Nicolai didn't say a word. But the one in front told Jesse: "Make a left."

They came past the control towers and the man said: "Runway four."

In the distance, Nicolai saw a Boeing 707. The curious thing about it was that it had no airline colors, no Air Force insignia. On the tail fin was a small Stars and Stripes, and there were some registration letters. But no other clue to the plane's identity: civilian, military, or private. It was anybody's guess.

Gail, who had been strangely subdued, spoke for the first time since they had reached the base. "That's yours," she said.

It seemed to put a sudden distance between them. Yours. Not ours. From now on, you're on your own.

"You are coming with me?" Nicolai said anxiously.

"Do you want me to?" she asked.

"What do you think?" He wanted to say he depended on her, he wanted her, he relied on her being with him. She gave him a rather sad smile.

"Don't worry," she said. "They booked me a seat too."

"Otherwise it's all off. I won't go," said Nicolai, trying to make it sound half joke, half serious.

The man next to him gave him a sidelong glance. The raincoat and the jacket were unbuttoned, and he saw the strap of a shoulder holster.

"Here we are," said Jesse, and the station wagon slid to a halt next to the gangway leading up to the 707.

They all got out. One of the two men ran up the steps into the plane. The other hovered around Nicolai.

"I'll have your gun, please," he said pleasantly to Nicolai.

He wasn't even surprised they knew he had the Makarov on him. Without a word, he took out the pistol and gave it to the man.

"Thank you, sir," the man said, and put it in his rain-coat pocket. He was painfully correct.

"Where are we going?" asked Nicolai.

"You're going home, Nick," said Gail.

Momentarily he panicked, and she must have seen his reaction, for she hastily added: "Your new home."

The plane was virtually empty; an Air Force officer with a briefcase sat in the first-class compartment, but he stared at them with such open curiosity that Nicolai guessed he didn't actually know who they were. He reckoned the officer was a courier, hitching a ride on the plane.

The man who had led the way into the plane showed him and Gail into first-class seats.

"Is this all right?" he asked Nicolai like a steward.

His colleague had also come on board and the two sat down a couple of rows to the rear of them. The first-class compartment was curtained off from the rest of the plane, but Nicolai sensed that there were no other passengers on board.

Almost immediately the seat-belt and no-smoking signs came on. It was rather like a ghost aircraft; he hadn't seen any crew at all.

"I hope we have a pilot," Nicolai said to Gail as she fastened her belt around her slim waist.

"We'll soon find out," she smiled back at him.

Unlike every civilian flight he had ever made, the plane began to taxi almost as soon as they were settled in. It seemed to have some kind of takeoff priority.

"You know, I haven't even got my toothbrush," said Nicolai.

Gail said something in reply, but it was drowned out by the sudden power thrust of the jet engines as the Boeing took to the air.

"What did you say?" he yelled, but she shook her head.

Now they were airborne, and the plane leveled off. Below them spread the German countryside, the thin spaghetti that was the autobahn network, the snakelike rivers, the patchwork fields. He could see a Rhineland castle, like a tiny cake decoration.

"Did you bring your passport?" Gail asked, surprisingly.

"Yes, as a matter of fact," said Nicolai.

"A real one?" Her eyes were mischievous.

"Gilt-edged diplomatic," he said. "But I haven't got a ticket!"

"That's no problem, Nick. From now on you travel at government expense. Our government!"

The seat-belt sign went off. They unclicked. Nicolai stretched himself.

"You know, it's a wonderful feeling," he said. "Just to sit here. With you. On this plane. To realize I've made it."

"It must be," said Gail, a little noncommittal.

The curtain to the rear compartment was pulled aside, and a stewardess in a white jacket appeared. She was a WAF, and she carried a tray with a coffeepot and several cups.

"You see, there *is* a crew," said Gail, seeing his reaction.

The stewardess came straight to their seats.

"Coffee?" she asked Gail.

"With cream, please."

She poured out a cup, and turned to Nicolai. "Coffee for you, sir?"

"I'd rather have a drink," said Nicolai, "if that's possible."

"Certainly, sir," said the stewardess. She had freckles and looked like a kid from the country. "What would you like? Whiskey? Vodka?"

Vodka! Did she know who he was? Or was it just coincidence?

"Martini. Very dry," ordered Nicolai.

"Thank you, sir," she said, and disappeared behind the curtain.

Gail lit a cigarette.

"Tell me," said Nicolai, "this plane. It belongs to the agency?"

"It's a government plane," said Gail.

"We have a fleet of our own aircraft in my organization," said Nicolai.

"Really?" She was curiously tense.

The WAF stewardess reappeared. "Your martini, sir," she said. It had two olives.

Nicolai took a sip.

"Ah, I needed that," he sighed. "Don't you want one?"

"Not at the moment," said Gail.

He frowned. "What's the matter? Is it the man who was killed? Karstetter?"

"His wife's just had a baby," she said.

"I'm sorry."

"He knew the risk. And it might have been you instead."

"That doesn't make it any better," said Nicolai.

"No."

He took another taste of martini.

"Where are we going?" he asked.

"I've no idea," she said. "That side isn't my department. You're going to the United States, that's all I know. They wanted you out of Germany as quickly as possible."

He screwed up his eyes. She was strangely fuzzy.

"You all right?" he asked.

"Yes. Just a bit worn out, I guess. It's been a long day." There were three Gails sitting next to him.

He put the glass on the tray between them. His hand was unsteady.

"I . . . I think . . ." he began, and then everything went black.

Arrival

Nicolai opened his eyes, and groaned. His temples throbbed, his head felt empty. He was disoriented. He had a crick in his left shoulder, having fallen into an awkward slump in his seat. The steady hum of the jet engines accompanied the return of consciousness as he shifted his body.

"Did you sleep well?" asked Gail. She was smiling at him. She had put on fresh lipstick, and he got a whiff of her perfume.

"What happened?" Nicolai asked thickly.

"You had a good nap," she said brightly. "You needed it. You were worn out."

He sat up straight. "You doped me," he said. "Why?"

"They thought you were very tense. They wanted you to relax. It was only a little sleeping pill."

"The hell it was," he said, feeling his head. "What a damn liberty. You could have told me. . . ."

"And you wouldn't have taken it," she said.

"It's the routine, is it?" he asked.

"Routine?" She blinked. "What routine?"

"Come on, Gail. With defectors? On a long journey?"

95

She tried to make light of it. "You know your trouble, Nick: you're too suspicious."

He glanced out of the cabin window. It was dark outside.

"What the hell's the time?" he said.

"We land in twenty minutes," said Gail.

So he had been out for hours. They had crossed the Atlantic while he was dead to the world. And that's how they had wanted it. To black him out. To give him less time to ask her questions. And less time to think about the reception that awaited him.

The freckle-faced Air Force hostess appeared with coffee. He took a cup gratefully.

"Would you like a Danish, sir?" she asked.

"No," said Nicolai. He needed the hot, strong coffee, but his stomach was churning. Whatever pill they had given him, he didn't like it.

"Where are we landing?" he inquired.

"I'm not quite sure."

"Eh?" He stared at her.

"The weather," she said vaguely. "I think they may have diverted us while you were asleep."

The two identical men had taken off their jackets, and were sitting together, playing cards. Nicolai saw the shoulder holsters. One of them looked at his watch and said something to the other. They put away the cards, stood up, and put on their jackets.

"Gail."

She looked at him.

"You remember what I asked you? You're not going to disappear, are you? After we've arrived?"

She shook her head. "Not if you don't want me to."

"It's important," he said.

"You're getting unprofessional, Mr. Galov."

"To hell with being professional," he said. "Maybe that's why I'm doing all this. At long last, I no longer want to be professional. I just want to be myself. Nicolai Galov. Plain mister. Highly unprofessional Mister Galov. You understand?"

"I think so," she said softly.

"The devil with the past. It is now the future that matters." He was speaking in a low voice, but rapidly, intensely. "The past no longer exists. I think you can help me to find the future. Please."

"You don't really know me, Nick," she said.

"Ah, that's where you are so wrong, dear Gail. I know you better than you think. And that night . . . that night in Frankfurt. I do not believe that was simply in the line of duty. . . ."

"That . . . that . . ." She stopped. "That was just . . . an incident, Nick. It's best we both forget it."

"On the contrary," he smiled very boyishly. "I want many more such incidents with you, Gail."

The lights overhead started flashing.

"You'd better put your seat belt on," she said. She glanced nervously at the two men across from them.

"Of course." He was very cheerful. "It would be tragic if we broke our necks after all this."

The plane began to descend, and he looked at her. She was staring straight ahead, then for a moment she turned her head and gave him a quick smile.

Nicolai braced himself for the touchdown.

Maryland

Nicolai didn't know they had landed at Andrews Air Force Base. The Boeing taxied to a remote runway, and when the door of the plane opened, one of the two identical men was first down the gangway. Gail followed, and then the only other passenger, the officer, clutching his briefcase.

Nicolai stood in the gangway, uncertain when to move until the second man said to him:

"Go ahead."

He started toward the door, the other man following close behind, like a bodyguard or an escort—or was it a prison warden?

At the top of the steps, Nicolai stood still for a moment and breathed the night air. It was a big airfield, with shadowy outlines of buildings in the distance and aircraft parked all around. It looked, in the dark, like a replica of Rhine-Main, which they had left eight hours earlier. Nicolai tried to find a clue to where they were—a control-tower sign, a name, anything—but there was nothing to help him.

At the bottom of the gangway were two black cars and a group of men. Gail stood with them and they all stared at him as he descended. Then a man with a mustache stepped forward.

"Welcome to the United States, Mr. Galov," he said. "This way, please."

He held open the door of one of the cars. Nicolai stopped. He looked at Gail.

"Is she coming?" he asked. She waved but didn't move. The men with her kept staring at him, expressionless.

"Please," said the man with the mustache. He gave Nicolai a gentle nudge. "It's only a short ride."

Nicolai got into the car, the man climbing in after him.

"My name is Spence," he said as they settled back. "It's good to have you here."

The car purred into action, and as it drew away from the group, the other car followed it, like a chaperone. Nicolai gave a final glance at Gail through the window. she had a firm, set, automatic smile on her face. He tried to imprint the look of her—her hair, her figure—on his mind like a photograph he would often have to rely on.

"Where are we going?" Nicolai asked, and shivered slightly.

"Are you cold, Mr. Galov?" said Spence solicitously. "We won't be long."

The car ride lasted only two or three minutes, and then they drew alongside a helicopter. Like the 707, it had no markings other than some registration letters and a big white "7" on the fuselage. It was painted black or dark blue, Nicolai couldn't tell which in the darkness, and there were some marines standing around.

"In you go, Mr. Galov," said Spence.

Nicolai hesitated. Then he climbed into the copter, followed by Spence. One of the identical men was already in the cabin, and Nicolai tried to figure out how he had managed to get there before them. He could see the vague figure of the pilot. He too seemed to be in marine uniform.

"You ever flown in one of these things?" asked Spence conversationally.

"Yes," said Nicolai.

"What would we do without them," Spence remarked as if it made them members of an exclusive brotherhood.

They settled back, and the helicopter took off amid the roar of its engines. The noise was so loud that conversation was difficult. But Spence put his head together with the other man, and said something. They looked at their watches, and the other man nodded.

Nicolai looked out of the cabin as the helicopter began to rise and then started flying at a surprisingly fast speed. They weren't more than a thousand feet off the ground, Nicolai judged as they passed over freeways, over streams of traffic, and across several localities. Not once could Nicolai spot a hint of where they were.

After a quarter of an hour, the bright lights below became fewer, and there were just one or two highways.

"Nearly there," shouted Spence.

Then the helicopter slowed down, and gradually it got lower and lower. Spread down below them was a wood, or so it seemed to Nicolai, and in the middle of it was a house with a big lawn.

The pilot in front was talking on the radio, but it was impossible to hear what he said. The helicopter hovered for a few moments, and then it started to descend.

"Here we are," Spence shouted, and smiled cheerfully at Nicolai.

There were lights in the house, and a figure stood on the lawn. They grew bigger and bigger, until the big machine touched down on the lawn.

The identical man opened the door and Spence indicated to Nicolai to follow him. Nicolai jumped out onto the grass. Behind him came Spence.

The figure that had been standing, watching them land, strode forward and held out his hand.

"At last," he said. "It's been a long wait, hasn't it?"

"I've been looking forward to it, too," said Nicolai. "How are you, Mr. Bishop."

Safe House

Bishop's expression did not change.

"You must have some good pictures," he said.

"We have."

"I'd love to read my dossier," said Bishop.

"And I'd like to read the one you have of me," replied Nicolai.

They measured up one another briefly, neither man disguising his inspection of the other.

"Let's go inside, Nick," Bishop said at last. He put his arm around Nicolai. "Come, I'll show you."

They walked over to the house. Its front door was open. Standing in the hall was a marine, with a belted holster.

Spence followed them inside, and the Marine shut the front door.

"No luggage?" asked Bishop.

"I got out rather quickly," said Nicolai. The entrance hall was impressive, with a staircase, wooden paneling, and a grandfather clock. It looked like the country retreat of a very rich man.

"Ah, yes, I forgot," said Bishop. He saw Nicolai looking around. "I thought you might stay here for a few days. You'll be made very comfortable, I promise you, and it's nicely out of the way."

"I'm sure," said Nicolai. "Where am I, actually?"

"You're very safe," was all Bishop replied.

He took Nicolai into a room off the hall. A log fire was blazing in the grate, and a table had been laid for two.

Bishop led the way and shut the door behind them. Nicolai caught a glimpse of Spence going up the stairs before the door shut.

"You need a drink, I guess," said Bishop. But he didn't even ask Nicolai what kind of drink he wanted. He walked over to the little cocktail bar and started to mix a martini. He was well briefed.

"It's been a very long day for you," he went on as he handed Nicolai the drink. "I imagine all you want to do is go to bed. We can have a quick snack if you like, and then I'll leave you alone."

He was like a considerate host, making a welcome guest feel at home.

"I had plenty of sleep on the plane," said Nicolai drily.

"Oh yes, of course." He nodded. "Well, don't worry. My martinis are straight. Cheers."

As they each took a sip, their eyes locked for a moment.

Bishop put his glass down. "Shall we have something to eat?" he suggested.

"When do we start, Mr. Bishop?" said Nicolai, a little harshly.

"Start?" Bishop feigned puzzlement.

"My debriefing. The interrogation."

"Oh *that*," said Bishop, as if it were the most unimportant thing in the world. "I wouldn't worry about it. Anyway . . ." He paused. "Maybe it's already started, don't you think?"

"Of course," Nicolai smiled thinly. "That is how we would do it, too."

"It might get a little more formal tomorrow," said Bishop. "As you know, there are certain procedures in these . . . cases."

Suddenly there was a loud, heavy throbbing noise from outside and the room shook slightly.

"It's only the chopper going home," explained Bishop. "Relax."

There was nothing to be seen of the outside. Heavy damask curtains had been drawn across the windows.

"Would you mind if I did go to bed now," said Nicolai. "I think you're right. I had forgotten my time clock."

He yawned and immediately excused himself.

"Surely," said Bishop. "But you must be hungry. You haven't eaten for eighteen hours."

Neat, thought Nicolai. Very neat. Telling me you know to the second when I had my last meal. And you're right. It was eighteen hours ago.

Aloud he said: "I'll take a sandwich and a glass of milk, please. I'll have it in bed."

"You're probably right," said Bishop. "I'll see to it. I'll get them to show you upstairs."

He opened the door. Spence was outside.

"Take Mr. Galov to his room," Bishop instructed. He turned to Nicolai. "Spence here is your right hand. Anything you want, any problem, anything at all, just tell him. See you in the morning."

"This way, Mr. Galov," said Spence.

Nicolai followed him up the stairs as Bishop stood in the hall, watching.

It was a comfortable bedroom, with its own bathroom. Both had the impersonal air of a hotel, and as in a first-class hotel there were a lot of amenities. Not only soap and towels, but also things he needed. Toothbrush, pajamas, slippers, a bathrobe. In his size too.

He opened the drawers, and found two sets of underwear, shirts, socks. All in his size.

"If there is something you need, just pick up the phone," said Spence. The phone had no dial.

"Thank you."

"Good night, Mr. Galov," Spence said, and closed the door.

Nicolai sat down on the bed and tried to figure out the next moves in the chess game that was being played around him. There was a knock on the door.

"Yes," said Nicolai.

It was a plate of sandwiches and a glass of ice-cold milk, on a tray carried by a marine.

"Turkey. Is that all right, sir?" asked the marine. He wore a sharpshooter's badge.

"Fine," said Nicolai.

"Anything else I can get you, sir?" asked the marine.

Nicolai looked hard at him, but if there were any other meaning to his question, the scrubbed-looking pink face under the regulation Corps crewcut belied it. What do they tell these fellows? Nicolai wondered. Did they know whom they were serving? Did this clear-eyed boy know he was a KGB defector? How did they pick them for this assignment?

"No, that'll be all," said Nicolai.

"Very good, sir," said the marine.

He shut the door quietly. Nicolai listened for the sound of a key being turned, a click, anything that indicated that he was locked in.

There was no telltale sound. But Nicolai knew without even looking that outside his door stood a Marine guard. A guard with a gun.

The Watch Room

In the basement, they sat at a tier of television screens. The closed-circuit system had every room in the house under surveillance, but Spence stood behind the shirt-sleeved technician who was watching the picture the concealed camera was feeding them from Nicolai's room.

They saw Nicolai reach for the glass of milk and take a couple of sips.

"He doesn't trust us, sir," said the technician, amused.

"Would you?" Spence asked. "In his shoes."

Nicolai got up from the bed and began to move around the room. They saw him slightly separate the curtains of the window overlooking the grounds. Then he glanced up at the ceiling, and at the air-conditioning vent, but if he knew that he was staring straight into the camera's lens, he gave no indication.

He took off his jacket, flung it over the back of the chair. Then he prowled around the room, looking at the walls, peering behind the framed picture of the New York skyline. He stooped, and felt under the bed, the chairs, the chest of drawers.

"What's the idea?" said the technician. "He knows we're bound to have surveillance equipment on him."

"Force of habit," Spence said, and pulled a stool over to sit beside the technician. "It's the routine and it dies hard."

"If he spots anything, what will he do then?"

"Nothing," said Spence. "But he'll sleep happy."

The technician grunted, and adjusted a dial. A second screen lit up. They had brought another hidden eye into action.

"Maybe," he said, "he's just telling us that he knows we know that he knows."

"You're taping the visuals?" asked Spence sharply.

"Sure," said the technician. He had last worked for the agency in Helsinki, and he was an expert in electronic surveillance. "But it'll be a waste of time, you'll see."

"Keep it going," ordered Spence. "Keep it going all night. If he even turns over, I want a picture of it."

"It'll be a waste of good videotape," grumbled the technician.

"Mr. Bishop's orders," said Spence, getting up from the stool. "If Tovarich so much as blinks an eyelid, he wants it on record. Understand, Harry?"

"Big shot, is he?"

"Just keep watching," said Spence.

Washington

The Admiral stood up behind his impressive desk as an aide ushered Gail into the office.

"Sit down, Mrs. Howard," he invited. He came around from his desk, and sat down in the deep armchair opposite her.

She *is* a very attractive woman, the Admiral decided. Her husband must have been quite something if she still carried a torch for him six years after he had been killed.

When she had first volunteered for covert work, there were some in the agency with strong reservations. A woman fighting her own private war, seeking revenge against those who had been her man's enemies, was dangerous. Emotional. Liable to let her feelings run away with her.

But she had connections. An uncle on Capitol Hill. Her family had pull. She spoke German and French fluently. The word came from on high: use her.

"I wanted to tell you myself how pleased we are with your work on Pheasant," he said. "In the best traditions of the service. Well done, Mrs. Howard."

"Thank you, sir." Her voice was low.

"Of course, Jack Karstetter's death is a tragedy. He was an excellent chief of station. We shall miss him."

She nodded.

"I wish sometimes that the people who denigrate our work would realize how many devoted, courageous agents we have. People like Jack. Giving their lives for their country without hesitation."

It was a speech worthy of a press conference. Then he came to the point: "I have studied the file. It makes very interesting reading. Tell me, have you any idea how they knew about the arrangement? How come they were there?"

"May I smoke?" asked Gail.

"Please," said the Admiral. But he made no move to light her cigarette. He was a courteous man, and polite to women, but he disapproved of smoking.

Gail lit her cigarette. "I don't know," she said. "I've been trying to work it out. I guess they must have followed him. . . ."

"A man like Galov would know how to shake them off," said the Admiral.

"If he spotted them. Can I ask you something, Admiral?"

"Of course."

"Why was there a twenty-four-hour delay in the pickup? He was already on the run. He was hiding out. We could have lifted him within a couple of hours. Right there in Frankfurt. Why did we wait until the next day, and set it up in Rudesheim, miles away?"

"Mrs. Howard," said the Admiral. "Operational details don't concern this office. Mr. Bishop knew what he was doing. He is an expert in these things." He smiled drily. "This is not the first defection he has processed, I assure you."

"And perhaps he was playing a little game. Maybe he wanted to see what the other side would do. So he gave them the time to do it . . . and it was Mr. Karstetter who was killed instead." She paused.

The Admiral was a master at dodging cross-examination.

"Why don't you ask Mr. Bishop?" he suggested.

"Maybe I will. One day."

The Admiral rose. She stubbed out her cigarette, and got up too.

"Anyway, Mrs. Howard, you've done very well. I think you deserve a little vacation. Any idea where you might be going?" He was watching her sharply.

Gail swallowed. "I hadn't even thought of taking leave. . . ."

"After a hazardous mission like yours, it's a good idea, believe me."

"I'll think about it," she said unwillingly. She hesitated. "How is he?"

"Who, Mrs. Howard?"

"Nicolai."

Her use of the first name alerted him. "Galov? He is being debriefed. These things take a little time."

"Is he all right?"

"Why shouldn't he be?" asked the Admiral coldly. "He is receiving the best of attention."

"I only wanted to know," she faltered.

The Admiral studied her with renewed interest. "What sort of man did you find him?" he inquired.

She sensed danger in his silky tone, and held tight to her Gucci bag.

"He's . . . a very pleasant man, I thought."

"How nice for you," the Admiral said, and held open the door for her.

In the corridor outside she wished she had had a chance to see what the file on his desk said about her.

Bonn

The Soviet Ambassador requested a meeting with the West German Foreign Minister at 11 A.M. "on a matter of some urgency."

The protocol office told the embassy that the Foreign Minister was "unfortunately not available at this time," but an undersecretary would be pleased to see the envoy at 3 P.M.

At 2:55 P.M. the Russian version of a Cadillac with its large red hammer-and-sickle ensign pulled up outside the VIP entrance of the West German Foreign Ministry.

"Thank you for seeing me at such short notice," said the Ambassador, sitting stiffly across from the undersecretary.

"The Minister apologizes for his absence, but regrettably he had a previous engagement," said the undersecretary. In fact, the Minister was dictating to his stenographer in another part of the massive building. "What can I do for Your Excellency?"

The Ambassador, as always, picked his words carefully. "This is really a domestic matter, but my government will appreciate any assistance you can give."

"Please go on."

"It concerns one of our officials in Frankfurt." He stopped, waiting to see if he could detect any reaction.

But all the undersecretary said was: "What seems to be the problem?"

"Vice Consul Nicolai Galov is missing. We would be grateful for your help in tracing him."

"Have you informed the appropriate authorities?" asked the undersecretary.

"Of course," said the Ambassador, "and the police are being very helpful. But we are anxious about Vice Consul Galov's state of health. The poor man may be in urgent need of help, and we feel it is imperative that he is found as quickly as possible."

The undersecretary was quite prepared to go through the routine. "You think he is ill?"

"It is possible he is suffering from amnesia," sighed the Ambassador. "We are very worried. He may be foundering around, not knowing who he is. He has been working very hard. And . . ." He paused.

The undersecretary waited politely.

"And there is also, I believe, some domestic problem. A matrimonial tiff. You know how it can be."

They exchanged men-of-the-world smiles.

"I'm so sorry," said the undersecretary. "How can we help?"

"All my government asks is that you take steps to insure that all your agencies have his description, and keep an eye open for the poor fellow."

"But of course," said the undersecretary.

The Ambassador smiled appreciatively. Then he cleared his throat.

"Needless to say, once you find Vice Consul Galov, we will take care of him."

This time he regretted his choice of words, because he thought the undersecretary gave him a rather sardonic look.

He was right. The undersecretary decided he might as well have some fun. "Have you considered, Ambassador, that perhaps Mr. Galov may no longer be within the jurisdiction of West Germany?"

"Anything is possible, Mr. Undersecretary. You will appreciate that our first concern is that no harm has befallen the vice consul."

The hell it is, thought the undersecretary.

"Have you announced his—er, disappearance publicly?"

"My government would prefer to keep this matter sub rosa," replied the ambassador. "It is, as I said, entirely a domestic situation. I take it that you have no information that might be of interest to us?"

"We are always the last to hear, Ambassador," said the undersecretary deprecatingly. "But it goes without saying that we will inform you immediately if anything comes to our notice."

"I am very grateful," said the Ambassador, "and I will immediately inform my government of your cooperation, which I know they will greatly appreciate."

After he had left, the undersecretary dialed a number on the private line.

"Doborev has just left, Minister," he said. "I think I ought to come and see you."

Safe House

Spence had taken Nicolai down to the room after breakfast. It was bare except for a table and two plain wooden chairs. The walls were painted green, and there were no windows.

"Make yourself at home," he told Nicolai, and left him on his own.

It was an interrogation room, no doubt about that. Nicolai had seen them before, but he had never been the object of the exercise. Now it was his turn.

The door opened, and a bald man in a blue blazer came in. His face was youthful, and his bald head did not go with it. He was carrying a black attaché case and a clipboard.

"How are you, Mr. Galov?" he asked cheerfully. He put the attaché case on the table and snapped open the lid. It looked vaguely like a hi-fi record deck, with a few extra dials and switches.

The bald man unwound a long lead, and plugged it into an electric point in the wall.

He sat down at the table opposite Nicolai, and put the clipboard in front of him.

"This is nothing to worry about," he said. "Just relax. I'm only going to ask you a few questions."

The lid of the attaché case blocked Nicolai's view, but he could see the man was adjusting various dials and switches.

Nicolai had expected this all along. "I'll take off my jacket," he volunteered.

"No need." He saw Nicolai's puzzlement. "No wires, I assure you. No electrodes. Don't worry about blood pressure or perspiration. That's all old hat."

Nicolai was professionally interested. "That's a very curious lie detector," he commented.

"Ah," said the man, like a scientist delighted to have found a kindred spirit. "You've got to forget about the old polygraph machines. I like to think of this little baby as the Supreme Test of Truth. I love it."

"Can I have a look?" asked Nicolai.

"Sure," said the bald man. "It's nice we got something your people haven't."

Nicolai walked around the table and studied the apparatus. It was beautifully compact.

"The IX-P," said the man proudly. "The Voice Stress Analyzer. She's beautiful. Aren't you, baby?" He beamed at Nicolai. "You see, she detects subaudible modulations in your voice patterns. She measures them and analyzes indications of psychological stress in the subject's voice that are quite beyond his ability to control. There's her own little computer. See it? It gives me an immediate digital readout. So simple. No charts to read, no graphs to decipher. I know immediately when a guy's lying."

This is absurd, thought Nicolai. Explaining to me the machine with which he was going to try and trap me if I give a wrong answer.

"Should you be telling me this?" he asked.

"Hell, Mr. Galov, I reckon you're an expert too. It's nice to show her off. And besides, there's nothing you can do about her. She knows her stuff."

"Supposing she's wrong about me?"

"She's never wrong, sir. The voice's subaudible modulations always tell the truth."

"Good," said Nicolai. "You'd better start asking."

"Well, you just sit down," said the bald man, "and take it easy, and answer whatever comes into your head. Just speak into this little mike." He had set it up in front of Nicolai.

"All set?" He smiled encouragingly.

Nicolai nodded.

"Let's see," mused the man. He studied the clipboard. "Your name is Nicolai Galov?"

"Nicolai Viktor Galov."

"A vice consul in the foreign service of the Soviet Union?"

"I was."

"Stationed in Frankfurt, West Germany?"

"I was."

"You are also an intelligence officer of the KGB?"

"I was."

The bald man looked up from the clipboard. "Listen, Nick, don't just keep saying 'I was.' You got to give the little lady here something to chew on. Okay?"

"Yes," said Nicolai.

"You were assigned to Special Service Section II of your directorate?"

"Correct."

"And what precisely were your duties?"

"You know what the section does."

"I'd like to hear your version."

"Well, I was involved in covert activities of various kinds."

"Would you be prepared to make a detailed statement, listing your missions, operations, your superior officers, and so on?"

"Of course."

"You're married?"

"Yes."

"But you did not bring your wife with you?"

"She is at home. I mean, in Moscow."

"Why did you not take her along?"

"I . . . we have had . . . our difficulties."

"Did she suspect that you were considering leaving her?"

"Who knows?"

"And you have your mother in the Soviet Union?"

"Yes."

"Aren't you afraid that they will be in danger because of your defection?"

"I don't think so. At least, I hope not. My mother is an old lady, the widow of a Hero of the Soviet Union. I don't believe they would take it out on her. And Shura—"

"Shura?"

"My wife. Shura's father has much influence. He is a colonel on the general staff—he knows all the right people—and Shura is a devoted Party member. The fact that she left me will speak for itself."

"You're doing very well, Nick," said the bald man.

"Is that all?" asked Nick.

"Heavens, no." He turned a page on the clipboard. "Ready?"

"Go on."

"Why have you come over to us?"

Nicolai was silent.

"Well?"

"I was thinking that the truth doesn't sound very good."

"Try us."

"You see, I simply want to get away from all this. That's the answer."

"All what?"

"All this. Interrogations. Suspicion. Double-dealing. Intelligence work. Counterespionage. Surveillance. Ciphers, codes. The whole damn apparatus. I'm tired, Mister . . . Mister . . ."

"Geiger," said the man. "Call me Jack."

"I know it isn't what you probably want to hear. That I love democracy, and want to live in a free country. Some of that is true, Jack, but really I just want out. I want to disappear, vanish into thin air, be rid of . . . of this whole darkness."

"Couldn't you just have quit?"

"Not back home. People like me are never allowed to get out. My only escape lay in defecting. I knew I'd have to put up with this kind of thing at first, debriefings, questions, cross-checks—but that once you got what you wanted, I'd be left to myself. Alone, obscure, unimportant. Do you understand?"

"And what have you brought us, Nick? Every hotel has a tariff, you know."

"Don't worry, I'll pay my way."

"Give me a little sample."

"No, that's for Bishop's ears."

"Listen, Nick, I assure you you can trust me."

"Jack, I'll tell Bishop. Okay?"

"Aren't you being a little cagey? Usually they pour their hearts out. At the first opportunity."

"They?"

"Defectors," said Geiger, and suddenly it sounded a nasty word. He examined the dials on the machine.

"I guess that's enough for now," he announced rather formally.

"Will I see you again, Jack?" asked Nicolai.

"I wouldn't be surprised," said Geiger. "I wouldn't be surprised at all."

Behind his genial demeanor, decided Nicolai, Mr. Geiger would make an ideal candidate for the Inspectorate.

Washington

The question came toward the end of the President's press conference.

"Mr. President," asked the man from the *Washington Post*, "it is rumored that a high official of the KGB has defected to the United States. Can you confirm this?"

"Perhaps you should put that to the KGB," said the President, amid laughter. He looked around expectantly for the next question, but the man from the *Post* was on his feet again.

"Mr. President, does that mean the rumors are correct, and that such a man has come over to us?"

The President was not pleased. His famous smile had faded. "The only information I have is that a Soviet Official abroad has asked for asylum in this country and his request is now being considered," he said.

"Is he already here?" asked the *New York Times*.

"I don't believe it would be helpful to add anything to what I have already said."

"Thank you, Mr. President," said the *Washington Post* politely.

The TASS correspondent waited impatiently for the press conference to finish. As soon as the President left the hall, he dashed from the White House.

Before he put the item on the wire to Moscow, he wanted to tell the embassy. Personally.

They would be very interested.

Safe House

"Names," said Bishop. "I want some names."

The room was hazy with cigarette smoke. They had both drunk half a dozen cups of coffee, and for once the immaculate Bishop's tie was a little loose and the top button of his shirt undone.

"I've had three debriefings now, Carl. Aren't you satisfied?" asked Nicolai wearily.

"Nick, you're doing fine," said Bishop. "All the stuff is very useful. You're giving us great insight into some things we're very interested in. Nobody's complaining. But I'd like you to finger a few people. You must know names, identities that we'd really like to hear."

"Maybe you wouldn't like to hear them."

"What does that mean, Nick?" asked Spence. He had been sitting in the corner, saying very little, just watching, listening.

"Well," said Nicolai, "here's a name for you."

Bishop and the other man tried hard not to look eager, but they didn't really succeed. They leaned forward, their eyes on his face.

"Eddie Haze," said Nicolai.

Bishop blinked.

"I told you you might not like it," said Nicolai.

"What about Eddie Haze?" demanded Bishop. Now he was cold, almost curt.

"Maybe you ought to take a good look at Mr. Haze," said Nicolai. "And not trust him quite so much."

"You wouldn't be playing games, would you, Galov?" Spence cut in. The atmosphere in the musty room had changed suddenly.

Bishop made an impatient gesture at Spence. "Are you saying he is a double agent?" he asked.

"Yes."

"Really? So why did you trust him? Why was he the one man you approached? Why did you hint to him that you wanted out? Why risk it, if you knew he was a double agent?"

"I didn't," said Nicolai. "Not then."

"But now you do?" Bishop's tone was sarcastic.

"Let me ask you something," said Nicolai. "Isn't it a strange coincidence that he just happened to catch the very bus to Rudesheim I had been told to take? That he just happened to travel with me all the way to the pickup? That Berezin was already there, waiting to kill me?" Nicolai's lips curled. "A very curious man, our Mr. Haze. Perhaps that's the trouble with freelancers in our work. They accept money from everybody."

There was a long silence.

Then Spence asked quietly: "Do you know for a fact that Haze worked for your people?"

"Of course not," said Nicolai. "I wouldn't have risked

dealing with him, would I? But now, after what's happened, I think it is, as you say, an educated guess."

"He's worked for Karstetter for years." Bishop shook his head. "Jack was no fool. And he trusted Eddie."

"Maybe that's why he is dead," said Nicolai.

Washington

The official note was delivered to the State Department at 11:32 A.M.

In it, the Soviet Government demanded the immediate return of Nicolai Galov, "who is being held against his will in the United States."

Information available to the Soviet Government, said the note, "suggests that Vice Consul Galov was kidnaped in Germany and taken to the United States by irresponsible elements apparently acting on the instructions of an official agency."

For good measure, the note added that Vice Consul Galov had not been well lately, and was "in urgent need of psychiatric treatment. His next of kin are anxious about his condition and have requested the Soviet Government to pursue his return home by the United States authorities with the utmost vigor."

Vice Consul Galov was about to be sent home "on extended leave to receive the care he needs" when he was kidnaped.

The Soviet Government had no doubt, purred the note, that the United States would not hesitate to comply with its request, and would not delay the handing over of this man.

At the same time, warned the note, it had to be pointed out that failure to comply would be regarded by the Soviet Government as "a provocation of a most serious nature," and the Soviet authorities cautioned that such failure would have "the gravest consequences."

"Well, what do you think?" the Secretary of State asked the Admiral.

"Bullshit," said the Admiral succinctly. "It's Formula 9. The usual routine when they want somebody who's escaped them."

"Did you kidnap him?" asked the Secretary of State.

"Mr. Secretary," replied the Admiral, looking hurt.

"He came begging. He asked to come over. You don't look a gift horse like that in the mouth."

"I hope he's worth all this," said the Secretary of State. He was due to meet the Soviet envoy socially at a UNICEF charity concert, and he didn't relish the idea of this damn thing coming up over a cocktail.

"We're busy debriefing him," the Admiral assured him. "It's proving very useful."

"How the hell did it ever leak out that we've got him?"

The Admiral shrugged. He hadn't been unhappy about the leak. After all, the Russians knew what had happened anyway. And it didn't do the agency's battered image any harm to pull off a little coup. Let the striped-pants boys in the State Department handle the waves. That was their job, after all.

"Trouble is," mused the Secretary of State, "now that everybody knows, we're stuck with him. We couldn't hand him back to the Soviets if we wanted to. Can you imagine the public outcry? That's all the President needs."

"I can see that," agreed the Admiral diplomatically.

"Just make sure of one thing," said the Secretary of State. "Keep the guy in cotton wool. Make sure nothing happens to him. I imagine they'd love to shut him up. So just make sure that nobody bumps him off. That's all we need."

In the elevator, the Admiral thought to himself how lucky it was that nobody knew about the four defectors who had been killed. So far nobody had linked the deaths, or who the victims were.

But the Secretary had been right, he reflected. Bishop had better make damn sure that Galov would not be No. 5.

Safe House

"You must be fed up with all this interrogation," said Dr. Harmer sympathetically. "Everybody asking you questions, and going over the same areas again and again."

The agency's psychiatrist had a soft, persuasive voice, which he controlled like a soloist in a symphony orchestra.

"I expected it," said Nicolai.

They were strolling on the grounds of the big house. They weren't alone; Nicolai knew that. In the distance, among the trees, he saw a Marine with a walkie-talkie. Other eyes were watching them too, he felt sure. But he was grateful to be in the open air.

"Here, boy," called out Harmer, flinging a ball for his Alsatian. He had brought the dog with him, and it danced attendance on them as they walked about.

"I don't have many opportunities to exercise him during the day," explained Harmer, half apologetically. "You don't mind, do you?"

"On the contrary," said Nicolai. He meant it. Seeing the dog streaking across the lawn made him aware of how trapped he felt about the four walls that were now virtually his whole world. "I envy him. . . ."

"Feeling cooped up, are you?" nodded Harmer.

"What do you think?" said Nicolai. "Oh, I can't complain about my treatment. The food's fine, I have books, newspapers, I can watch TV, my bed's comfortable, everybody is very polite, but . . ."

"But you feel a prisoner," said Harmer. "Most understandable. Still, it won't last forever. This is a necessary process." The dog brought the ball to him, proudly, and he flung it again as far as he could. "At the same time, I know you must resent it subconsciously. You know it has to be done, you expected it, as you say yourself, but you wouldn't be human if you weren't getting restless."

"Is that your psychiatric evaluation, Doctor?"

"Oh, that's much more complicated," said Harmer. He let that sink in, for effect, and was pleased when he saw Nicolai frown. "One thing I do know. You're lonely, Nick."

They walked in silence.

Then Harmer suddenly asked: "Do you miss your wife?"

"Well, I think of her sometimes; of course I do," said Nicolai. "But it was all over between us. We both knew it. It's a closed chapter."

"Is that why you still carry her photo around with you all the time?" asked Harmer.

Nicolai stopped. So they had looked through his wallet. They had never taken it from him, so they must have done it while he was asleep. They had found Shura's photo, and then put it back again.

"She is very pretty," added Harmer.

"Yes."

"What went wrong?"

Nicolai shrugged. "It's just one of those things. They happen."

"As a psychiatrist, I find that a very unsatisfactory answer," said Harmer. "But I will draw my own conclusions."

"Oh, really?"

"Don't worry about it," said Harmer, and he knew that was a very unsettling thing to say.

The dog ran up, panting, and rubbed its head against Nicolai's leg.

"Now, *that's* very unusual," said Harmer, startled. "He must like you."

Nicolai stroked the Alsatian's head. "It's nice to have one friend here," he said.

"My dear Nick, for all you know you have more than one," said Harmer.

He threw the ball again, and the dog pursued it.

"He's a lovely animal," said Nicolai.

"And he's a very good bodyguard," added Harmer unexpectedly.

"You need one?"

"Don't we all, in this business?" said Harmer.

They started to go back to the house.

"I must say, it was very nice of you to let me have those cassettes of Shostakovich and Khachaturian," said Nicolai. "It's much appreciated."

"If it makes you feel more at home, I'm delighted," said Harmer.

"I was surprised, actually."

"Why?" asked Harmer.

"The psychiatrists we use are great believers in alienation," said Nicolai. "The last thing they'd want to do with somebody like me is to remind him of home. I expected you to feed me disco music all day to Americanize me."

"Well, you're learning," said Harmer. "Maybe it proves I could never be a psychiatrist in the KGB."

He did not like Nicolai's smile.

"You must stop being so tense," urged Harmer. "Lower your defenses. Relax. Let yourself go. Now you're a free man, there is nothing to be afraid of."

"Isn't there?" asked Nicolai.

"We'll take good care of you."

Harmer's silk tie had slipped a little, and Nicolai saw the tiny clip-on microphone. They were recording everything.

But Nicolai gave no sign that he had even noticed.

It was Harmer who surprised him.

"You didn't mind, did you?" he said. "It's routine."

"Of course." Suddenly Nicolai liked him. "That's how we do it too."

Boston

The phone rang shortly before noon, but it might have been the middle of the night as far as the red-haired girl lying in bed was concerned. She hadn't gotten back to her apartment until 5 A.M. and she was still half asleep as she groped for the receiver.

"Hello," she managed to say, and yawned.

"Gerry, wake up," said the man's voice.

"Who's that?" she asked sleepily.

"Bob Spence."

Suddenly she was very much awake. She sat upright. She always slept naked, but that was not the reason she shivered slightly.

"Bobby," she cried, a little too enthusiastically. "Long time no hear."

"How's life?"

"I make a living," said the redhead. "You know how it is. Where are you?"

His answer was another question: "Are you alone?"

"Sure."

"And are you free tonight?"

"Try me."

She was surprised he even asked. Under the arrangement, she was always on standby, and if they wanted her, everything else went by the board.

"Got a little job," said Spence.

"Who is it?"

"We'll pick you up. You'll like him, Geraldine."

"What do I call him?"

Spence hesitated a moment. Then he said: "Nicky."

"That's cute," said the redhead. "What does he do?"

"Doesn't matter. Just look after him. And remember the rules. You don't know anything. And you forget about it afterward."

"Bobby, I don't need reminding."

"Okay then. Be ready at six."

118

"Sure thing." Her grip on the telephone receiver tightened. "Bobby?"

"What is it?"

Now she had plucked up courage, she went right into it: "How much?"

"The usual," he said coldly.

"I was wondering . . ." said the redhead. Her resolution was faltering.

"Yes?" Spence's tone was not encouraging, but she tried anyway:

"What about an extra five hundred?"

"Why?"

"Bobby, a girl's got to eat. I haven't had a raise . . . jeez, I don't know for how long. Everything's going up, and—"

He cut her short. "We got a contract with you, right, Geraldine?"

"Sure."

"Let's stick to it."

"Well . . ."

"Six o'clock sharp. Okay?"

"Okay," she said reluctantly.

The phone went dead.

She swung her legs onto the sheepskin rug in front of the big double bed. She padded, still naked, to the kitchen and put on the coffee. She needed it. Hot. Strong. Black.

She looked at herself in the long mirror in the bathroom. Her shape was great. With a body like that, she could have got far on her own. She was sure of that. So why the hell had she got herself involved with them? For the sake of the retainer?

She wished she had never heard of them. Because, knowing them as she did now, there was no way of getting out.

Motel

The limousine's black curtains were drawn. Nicolai wondered if it was to stop people from looking in at him or to stop him from looking out.

"Well, Nick, how does it feel to be out and about at last?" asked Spence.

"I feel like a prisoner being taken to a new jail," said

119

Nicolai bitterly. "Why all this?" He nodded at the curtains.

"Insurance," said Spence.

"Against what?"

"Don't be naïve," said Spence. He reached inside his jacket and pulled out a wad of fresh, crisp dollar bills.

"Five hundred," he said, holding it out. "Take it."

"What for?"

"To enjoy yourself. Hell, you deserve a night out."

"And where can I spend it?"

Spence pushed the money into his hand. "You'll find a way." He winked.

"Whose idea is all this?" asked Nicolai stiffly.

"R and R," said Spence.

"Please?"

"Rest and Recreation. A guy needs R and R. You've been under pressure, Nick. Questions, questions, the same four walls. A fellow can do with some fresh air when he's been going through what you have."

"Do I thank Dr. Harmer for this?" said Nicolai.

"Thank the U.S. taxpayer."

Nicolai laughed.

"What's so funny?" asked Spence suspiciously.

"I was just thinking, how amazingly alike they are, your organization and mine. Perhaps we use the same manual and don't even realize it. Do you know, we do it exactly the same way. When we have somebody under intensive examination, we suddenly give him a little treat. It's quite unexpected, and comes as a great surprise to the subject. Tell me, who's my swallow?"

"What the hell are you talking about?" said Spence, rather sourly.

"My comforter. My little friend. We call them swallows. Our ladies of the night. Providing companionship, softness, relaxation. Who have you picked to be my—playmate?"

Spence was indignant. "You make us sound like a bunch of pimps, Galov. Damnit, you got the wrong country. We don't do such things. You think Congress would give us funds to lay on—well, that kind of thing? What you do is your business, but we don't have any part of it. You got to learn, buddy."

"My mistake," said Nicolai, but he was still smiling.

Spence sat back in the car and sulked.

"Please," said Nicolai. "I understand your position, believe me. I've had to do this kind of thing. It can be very funny. You remember Bergstrom?"

Spence was interested. "The Swedish Air Force lieutenant who got fifteen years? What about him?"

"My department set him up, so to speak. We wanted pictures."

"Yeah, I remember. To blackmail him."

"Well," said Nicolai. "They provided a little swallow for him, and left them to it. But the case officer had got it all wrong. Our handsome blond Swede wasn't interested in pretty little swallows."

"Well?"

"I had to make sure he met somebody nearer his inclinations. It was most distasteful, and I was glad to leave them to it." He shook his head. "But it had its funny moments."

"If you say so."

The glass pane that divided them from the driver slid silently down.

"You want me to stop outside, sir?" asked the driver. He was in civilian clothes, but his crewcut spelled marine all over.

"Why not?" said Spence.

The limousine stopped, and the driver opened the door.

They were in front of a motel alongside a country road off the main highway. A blue neon sign proclaimed DICK'S MOTEL, but there was another electric sign stating NO VACANCIES.

"Come on," said Spence.

The man behind the reception desk was reading a newspaper, but he stood up when they came in.

"Good evening, Mr. Spence," he said. They seemed to know each other. He reached into a pigeonhole behind him and brought out a key.

"Bungalow 3, Mr. Robinson," he said to Nicolai. "Hope you enjoy your stay."

"This way," said Spence. Nicolai followed him outside again. The limousine was still parked in front with the driver standing beside it. Spence led Nicolai to a small bungalow thirty yards away.

"Have a nice time, Nick," he said, and handed him the key. "If you want transportation, just call the desk. I'll pick you up after breakfast."

He walked off. The bungalow's curtains were drawn, but Nicolai could see chinks of light from inside.

He unlocked the door.

Soft music was playing and a red-haired girl came toward him with a welcoming smile.

"Hi, Nicky," said Geraldine.

Washington

"Well, how did they get on?" asked Bishop.

"The tape makes interesting listening," said Spence.

Bishop reacted with disgust. "I'm not into that sort of thing, Bob," he said curtly.

"If that's what you're thinking, you're wrong," said Spence. "You know what they did? They spent all night talking, and they got very, very drunk. That's all. When I picked him up in the morning, Galov had the biggest hangover you've ever seen."

"They *talked?*" frowned Bishop. "All night? What about?"

Bishop looked at his little memo pad.

"Well, if you want to know, Hemingway, the Spanish Civil War, bullfighting, Raymond Chandler, supermarkets, Nixon, Dostoevski, and suicide. In that order, roughly."

"I don't believe it," groaned Bishop.

"It's all on tape."

"Hemingway? Dostoevski?" Bishop was bewildered. "She talked about *them?*"

"They had an interesting discussion," said Spence. "She has some strong views on the stylistic differences between them."

"Just what kind of girl did you pick, damnit?" snarled Bishop. He hated the unexpected.

"Our Geraldine majored in literature, it turns out," said Spence, somewhat sheepishly. "She is much more intelligent than I gave her credit for. . . ."

"Great, just great. You mean they never went to bed?"

"In a way, they did."

"Ah."

"They lay on the bed, getting soused out of their minds. In the morning, before he left, Galov gave her a kiss, said how much he had enjoyed talking with her, and gave her the five hundred bucks."

Bishop was impatiently drumming his fingers on his desk.

"I know, Carl, the guy doesn't sound human," said Spence hurriedly. "I don't get it. He likes women. Gerry is a real dish too . . ."

Bishop had acquired the Admiral's habit of doodling. He was abstractedly drawing on a piece of paper. Suddenly he asked: "She doesn't know who he is?"

"No."

"And he didn't let anything slip?"

"Nothing that ties in."

Bishop threw down his pencil.

"You think it was all a waste of time, do you, Bob?"

"It looks like it, doesn't it?" said Spence uncomfortably.

"I think it's very interesting. It was all done for our benefit, you would say? And yet I wonder . . ."

"I don't get you, Carl."

"Your Russian is very moral. He is not promiscuous. He is very strict, almost puritanical."

"Oh, come on. You make him sound like Superprig. The guy's flesh and blood."

"They can be very old-fashioned in our eyes," said Bishop. "Especially when they're in love."

His eyes narrowed.

"You know, maybe our friend has just betrayed himself."

Safe House

"Mr. Sondergard is from the State Department," said Bishop.

The gray-haired man in the dark suit with the club tie gave Nicolai a friendly nod. "It's very good of you to see me," he said courteously.

Nicolai felt like telling him: Don't play such a silly game. Would I refuse? Could I refuse?

The way it had been put to him he had no choice anyway. His presence was required, and nobody asked him how he felt about it.

"I will come straight to the point, Mr. Galov," Mr. Sondergard said. "The Soviet Government has requested that you be returned to Russia."

He waited for a reaction. "Yes" was all Nicolai said.

"I am sure that this will come as no surprise to you," purred Mr. Sondergard. "It does mean, though, that I have to ask you quite formally whether you wish to be handed back to them?"

"I hardly want to sign my own death warrant," said Nicolai.

"Quite so." Mr. Sondergard was like an Englishman. He was the most un-American character Nicolai had met so far. His suit could have come from Savile Row, his gray hair seemed trimmed by a Jermyn Street barber, and his accent was the product of Oxford.

"I must tell you that the Soviet authorities say that you have nothing to fear if you return. They in fact say they wish to care for you as they claim that you are probably in need of treatment. That is what they say. They have mentioned amnesia."

"Of course," said Nicolai.

"My understanding," Mr. Sondergard went on, "is that you have been examined both medically and psychiatrically since you arrived over here and that, I am happy to say, the verdict is there's nothing wrong with you." He looked at Bishop for confirmation. The nod he got satisfied him. "Nevertheless, you must be the final judge."

"You mean, you want me to say that I don't think I'm crazy?"

Mr. Sondergard raised a well-manicured hand. "Mr. Galov, it is essential that we observe the proprieties with the Soviets to a tee. Suggestions have been made that you are being held against your will, that you were kidnaped, and that we are detaining you by force. You repudiate that?"

"I am here of my own free will," replied Nicolai.

"And you confirm that if your whereabouts are secret, and you are guarded, it is for your own protection, and not to restrain you?"

"That's right." Nicolai glanced at Bishop. "Isn't it?"

"Mr. Sondergard," said Bishop, "the Department of State can be assured that whatever measures we have taken are purely in the interests of Mr. Galov's security."

"Of course." Mr. Sondergard cleared some phlegm that had been bothering him. "Now, Mr. Galov, it is correct, is it not, that you wish to remain in the United States?"

"I would not be here otherwise."

Mr. Sondergard paused. He was going over the formula in his mind. "You realize, of course," he said at last, "that your exact alien status over here has still to be determined."

"Wait a moment." Nicolai clenched his fist. "Are you trying to say you . . . you're still not sure what will happen to me? You haven't made up your mind?"

"Easy, Nick," said Bishop. "These are formalities. They've got to work out what you are. A refugee? A political fugitive? An immigrant? It's paperwork. Don't worry about it?"

Nicolai stood up, white-faced.

"Paperwork?" he cried. "It's my life you're talking about. I asked for sanctuary. Don't you understand?"

"Sit down, Mr. Galov," said Mr. Sondergard, not unkindly. "Of course we realize your situation. But sanctuary is not really a legal term. These things have to be processed. . . ."

"Processed, processed—I hate that word," shouted Nicolai. "I haven't stopped being processed. Twenty-four hours a day. When do I stop being processed and become a free human being?"

"Take it easy, Nick," said Bishop. "We're all trying to help you. But you must help us."

Nicolai sat down. "I'm sorry," he said. "I've been through a lot."

"For the record, it is necessary for me to put this to you," said Mr. Sondergard. "Were you in any way solicited by the United States Government to desert your post and turn yourself over?"

The record was the black box on the desk, taping every word they said.

"No," said Nicolai. "No. I . . . I wanted to."

"You see, the Department has to have an absolutely watertight case, and must have all the answers ready," said Mr. Sondergard. "We do not wish your—er, defection to . . ." He stopped, then continued: "You will appreciate that we do not want this affair to put an undue strain on U.S.–Soviet relations."

"Don't worry, Nick," interrupted Bishop. "That doesn't mean we'd hand you back. . . ."

"Good," said Mr. Sondergard. "That's that, then. Now let's get to the point."

Nicolai tensed.

"The Soviet Embassy has demanded a confrontation with you. They insist that they want to see you face to face, and to hear from your own lips what you have just told me." Mr. Sondergard pursed his lips. "I know this might be a strain for you, and I can advise you that you can refuse to have such a meeting." He paused.

"Yes," said Nicolai dully.

"At the same time, we would urge you to go through this ordeal. It would be the strongest way to silence their propaganda machine. As long as you remain concealed from them, they will repeat the allegations that you are being held by force against your will. It is entirely up to you, but we would greatly appreciate your cooperation."

"You'll be perfectly safe," urged Bishop. "The meeting would take place at the State Department, and we would be there. You would not be left alone with the embassy people. It wouldn't take very long. How about it, Nick?"

"I hate the idea," said Nicolai.

"They can't do you any harm, and you'd never have to see any of them again."

"There is nothing to be afraid of, Mr. Galov," Mr. Sondergard assured him. "And the United States Government would be very grateful. It is a delicate situation, as you can imagine."

Nicolai stared out of the window while they sat silent, their eyes on his face.

"All right," Nicolai agreed at last. "I'll do it."

"A very good decision." Mr. Sondergard was pleased. "It will make everything very much easier."

"There is something else you should know, Nick," said Bishop.

Suddenly Nicolai felt very cold.

"Your wife is in the United States."

Nicolai sat motionless.

"Shura wants to see you."

"Here?" croaked Nicolai. "She is *here?*"

"We decided to accede to her request when she applied for a visa," said Mr. Sondergard. "It would have given the wrong impression to refuse."

"Incidentally," smiled Bishop, "Shura sends you her love. All her love."

Washington

They hustled Nicolai into a back entrance of the State Department offices with a blanket draped over his head.

"We don't want your picture on every front page in the country," explained Spence.

Nicolai was surrounded by the four unsmiling men who had escorted him to Washington. They had made the journey in two cars, black drapes once again hiding Nicolai. Spence rode in the lead car.

Inside the building, they removed the blanket. They had ridden up in an elevator and walked along a corridor. Now they were in an anteroom. Mr. Sondergard was already waiting.

"Did you have a good trip, Mr. Galov?" he asked. The journey had taken about three hours, by helicopter and limousine. Mr. Sondergard didn't really seem interested in his reply. He looked at his watch and said: "We have about fifteen minutes before they're due. How about some coffee?"

"Thank you," Nicolai said gratefully. He could use it. He hoped they didn't see how nervous he was.

"I might tell you we nearly had a problem," said Sondergard. "At the last moment they insisted that the meeting should be at the Soviet Embassy. Naturally we refused."

"Are you all right, Nick?" asked Spence anxiously. He had noticed the strained look.

"I'll be glad when it's over," replied Nicolai.

Spence was sympathetic. "I can well believe that."

"Let me give you gentlemen a quick rundown how we will play this," said Sondergard. He was carrying a black leather file folder, and Nicolai wondered what it contained. "It will be very informal. We will sit on one side of the table, with you, Mr. Galov. They will sit opposite us on the other side. They're sending Shagin, the minister at the embassy, and an attaché, Zakov."

Zakov. Nicolai froze.

"Fedor Zakov?" he asked sharply.

"You know him?"

"Oh yes," said Nicolai. "I know him, all right."

"Tell us about him," drawled Spence.

"You must know damn well who he is," snapped Nicolai angrily.

"We have a little file on him, but I'd like your version."

"Zakov is a most dangerous man. Most dangerous. I am surprised you allow him to be accredited to your government."

"Sometimes," said Spence, "it is useful to play along and know where they're located rather than having them drift around in unknown places."

"Anyway, he can do you no harm here." Sondergard's tone was reassuring. "You're perfectly safe."

"Nobody's safe with a reptile like Zakov around," said Nicolai.

"He was General Modin's assistant for some time, wasn't he? In your organization's inspectorate?"

"That's right, Mr. Spence."

"So you can see we're perfectly well informed," said Spence smoothly. "You can relax."

Sondergard coughed delicately. "They're bringing one other person with them," he said. "It may be a little painful for you, but there's nothing we can do, unless you refuse to see her. Your wife is coming."

"I expected it," said Nicolai calmly. "Once you told me she was here." He shrugged. "I might as well get it over, once and for all."

Sondergard nodded approvingly. "A very sensible attitude."

A tap on the door, and a young man appeared. He was a younger version of Sondergard, equally Ivy League, equally well dressed, and smooth-spoken.

"They've just arrived, sir," he said.

"Thank you, Jackson. Is everything set?"

"I'll have them shown to conference room D," said Jackson diffidently.

"Good. And let us know when you're ready for us."

"Of course, sir." Jackson took the opportunity to flash a quick, curious look at Nicolai before he disappeared as softly as he had entered.

"It'll soon be over and done with," said Spence. "It's just an exercise in diplomatic relations."

"Oh, sure," said Nicolai.

"I am sure they look on it the same way," added Sondergard.

Nicolai smiled sourly. He took another sip of coffee, but it had gone cold.

"Oh, one other thing," said Sondergard. Nicolai was getting used to his habit of always adding postscripts. "They may try threats and they may try blackmail. Don't give in to either. They're very anxious to have you back and they'll try all the pressure they can. . . ."

"You're wrong, Mr. Sondergard," said Nicolai. "They're not really anxious to have me back. But they're very anxious to have me dead."

Jackson appeared again.

"They're ready for you, gentlemen," he announced.

Spence noticed that Nicolai was sweating, but he didn't comment.

Conference Room D

The table in the room had been laid out as if for a summit meeting. There were six places, three on each side, with six legal note pads and six sharpened pencils.

In the center of the table were six glasses and two carafes containing ice water. On the walls were oil paintings of elderly gentlemen with side whiskers and demeanors of utmost gravity; Nicolai guessed they were nineteenth-century Secretaries of State.

But that was later.

All Nicolai had eyes for now was Shura. She was beautifully dressed. She had a raccoon fur coat on, and he was surprised she hadn't taken it off, for the room was warm. She had elegant shoes, the kind she couldn't buy in Moscow, and he could see the gold necklace that had been his wedding gift.

But she was pale. She had a different makeup on, and it seemed to emphasize her whiteness and the shadows under her eyes. She wore lipstick, but that too only served to accentuate her wan look. Her hands trembled slightly as they clutched a handbag.

And she was staring at him, right into his eyes, as if she had a thousand questions.

"Shall we be seated?" invited Sondergard. He had assumed the role of chairman and nobody challenged it. "Do you wish this to be on the record?" he inquired.

"That's not necessary," said Shagin. He was a scholarly man whose appearance matched his reputation as an outstanding linguist. He spoke a number of Arabic dialects convincingly, and his CIA file noted that he had played a sinister if little known role in tumbling the Shah while at the Soviet Embassy in Teheran.

Like Shura, Zakov kept his eyes fixed on Nicolai. He still had the little black beard he'd sported in Budapest. He was the only Soviet official Spence had ever seen who wore a bow tie.

"That's agreed, then," said Sondergard. "Now the purpose of this meeting—"

"Excuse me," interrupted Shagin mildly. "Who is that gentleman?"

"Oh, I am sorry." Sondergard was just as mild in manner. "Mr. Spence is present at the request of Mr. Galov. He is his adviser."

Nicolai shifted uncomfortably.

"Yes, Mr. Sondergard, but what is his status?" insisted Shagin.

"He is an official of the United States Government," said Sondergard.

"He is CIA," snapped Zakov.

"Oh really, gentlemen," protested Sondergard. "Can we get on?"

"It is not desirable that a member of the CIA should sit here to intimidate Mr. Galov," said Zakov. "His presence is a threat."

It only proved to Sondergard what the black leather file folder already had told him; that Zakov, a mere attaché, was senior to Shagin, the minister.

"Why don't you tell us what your job really is, Fedor?" said Nicolai.

"Please, Mr. Galov," snapped Sondergard. "I must ask you to restrain yourself." He put on his diplomatic mask again. "As I was saying, the reason for this meeting is that your government, gentlemen, wishes to convince itself that Mr. Galov is in the United States of his own free will and volition, and that you want to see him in person."

"Correct," said Shagin. He leaned across the table. "Nicolai Viktor, you can speak freely. We are here, and you are now free to tell the truth. You are perfectly safe at last. . . ."

"I seem to have heard that a couple of times lately," said Nicolai, glancing at Spence.

"We have come to take you back to the homeland," announced Zakov. "You are not well, Nicolai. You need treatment. You know you will have the best of care once you return. There is nothing seriously wrong with you, you just need good food and good rest, and the loving care of your wife and your mother."

Nicolai said nothing.

"Well, Mr. Galov?" inquired Sondergard.

"Tell them no thank you," said Nicolai. He saw Shura's troubled, pleading look.

"We only care for your welfare," said Shagin. "You were the victim of a piratical assault by illegal elements who kidnapped you and are holding you against your will."

Zakov nodded. "You are probably at this moment doped, and under hypnosis to stop you speaking the truth."

Sondergard became quite red with indignation. "That's an outrageous suggestion, sir," he exploded. "I must ask you to withdraw."

"But we are not on the record anyway, Mr. Sondergard," said Shagin. "Well, Nicolai? What do you say?"

"I came here voluntarily. No one forced me. It was my own decision. I wanted to come here."

"But why, Nicolai?" asked Shagin.

"You wouldn't understand if I explained it for two days," said Nicolai.

"Your mother misses you," volunteered Shagin. "The old lady is very unhappy. She doesn't understand how you could do such a thing to her. You, the son of a Hero of the Soviet Union. She wanted to be here herself to beg you to come back, not to bring disgrace on her, but she could not make the journey. The terrible shock has made her very ill. She keeps asking for you. Don't you miss your mother?"

"I miss her, very much. But in the long run, it is my life. . . ."

"That is very callous," said Zakov. "A son has a duty to his mother, just as you have a duty to your country."

"I do not need sermons from you, Zakov," said Nicolai.

They sat in silence, Shura clutching the edge of the table.

"Mr. Sondergard," said Shagin at last. "I wonder if the United States Government is aware of certain background about this man. Perhaps you will look on him in a different light if I tell you certain facts. This man is a criminal. He is not seeking sanctuary for any so-called ideological reasons, but simply to evade justice."

Shura started to open her mouth, but no sound came out.

"I am sure he has not told you that he murdered a man, and went on the run to avoid arrest."

Shagin looked at Zakov like a man seeking approval. And Zakov nodded.

"Who am I supposed to have murdered?" asked Nicolai quietly.

"Leonid. Leonid Dushkin. He died after your brutal and unprovoked attack on him in your apartment," said Zakov.

"No. He wasn't dead. . . ."

"He died in the hospital. You are a murderer."

"Now just a moment, gentlemen," began Sondergard. For the first time Spence spoke. "May I?" he asked.

"Go ahead."

"Mr. Galov has concealed nothing from us. In one of his debriefing sessions he explained how he had to put this man Leonid . . . out of action. You know very well what Leonid was. A KGB heavy. To make sure Mr. Galov got dragged back to the Soviet Union, at gunpoint if necessary. If the man subsequently died, I am sure Mr. Galov regrets it, but he was fleeing for his life."

"This is outrageous," cried Zakov. "It is slander. The American Government is harboring a murderer and we demand his extradition so that he can stand trial and receive his due punishment."

"I thought," said Sondergard mildly, "that you were only concerned about Mr. Galov's health, that you felt he had been abducted against his will, and that all you want for him is good care and a reunion with his family. . . ."

Zakov slammed his fist on the table.

"I warn you," he declared, "this can have serious consequences. The whole matter is a provocation by your CIA. By that man there . . ."

He pointed a quivering finger at Spence.

"Him and his fellow brigands."

Spence grinned at him, unashamedly.

"Gentlemen, I do not believe there is much point in continuing along these lines," said Sondergard in his mild style. "We have given you the opportunity to talk to Mr. Galov. You have heard him. I think that's as far as we can go."

"Correct," agreed Shagin. Zakov glowered at Nicolai.

"I have only one more request. A very human one," added Shagin. "I am sure you will understand. It is Mrs. Galov's wish that she be allowed to have a few minutes alone with her husband."

"With no one else present?" asked Spence sharply.

"It is a most reasonable request, and she has come a long way."

Sondergard brushed some invisible dust from the leather file. "Well . . ." he began. He turned to Spence.

"What do you think?"

"It's up to Mr. Galov, isn't it?" replied Spence coldly.

"How do you feel about it?" Sondergard asked Nicolai.

Nicolai looked at Shura and felt he could not have said no if his life depended on it, she looked so forlorn, pathetic, anxious.

"Yes," he said. His mouth was dry.

"Very well," said Sondergard. "We will leave you to it."

As he brushed past him, Spence whispered to Nicolai urgently. "Watch yourself. I'll be right outside. Just watch yourself."

But Nicolai hardly heard him. They closed the door and left the two of them alone.

For a moment they looked at each other across the table in silence.

And then Shura moved toward him.

Fort Meade

It took the computers two hours finally to decipher the "most urgent" short-wave message that had gone from Moscow to all stations, worldwide.

It made its point succinctly.

Nicolai Galov was to be terminated on sight.

The message wasn't addressed to any specific Soviet mission, but was an instruction to all posts, in all countries.

"They really must want him badly," said the chief of the special section that handled broken Soviet ciphers and codes. "I've never known them to broadcast a thing like this so widely."

"You mean, they want us to know," commented Bishop.

"We have no reason for thinking they're aware we have the ability to read this cipher," said the chief proudly. "As you know, we don't act on these messages, so we don't betray our deciphering skills to them. No, I guess Galov is dynamite. They're out to get him, no matter what it takes."

"Maybe you're right," Bishop muttered abstractedly.

What he was really interested in at that moment was happening in conference room D. He was very anxious to know how that little get-together was working out.

Conference Room D

She threw her arms around him. She was half-crying, half-laughing.

"Oh my darling," she sobbed, "I am so happy to see you."

She pressed herself close to him.

"Nicky, oh Nicky," she kept saying. Her pale face was tear-streaked, and she kissed him and held on to him as if she would never let him go.

"Shura," he said gently. He disengaged himself, and took both her hands. He guided her to a chair. "Please, dear, don't . . ."

She sniffed and pulled out a handkerchief, dabbed her nose.

He sat down next to her. "You look well," he lied.

"Come back with me," she pleaded. "It will be all right, I promise you. But please come back. I need you. Do you have any idea how much I've missed you?"

"Have you forgotten, Shura?" he asked softly.

Her green eyes widened. "Forgotten what?"

"Shura, my beautiful, it's too late. There is no turning back. Not for me. Not for you."

"I love you," she whispered, and he still felt the pain in his heart. "Please . . ."

"No," he said. "I want you to be happy, babushka, but I can't be that happiness. Things . . . between us . . . well, you know how it's been . . ."

"We can start again," she said eagerly. "I was stupid.

Bored. I didn't mean the things I said. I was a cow to you."

"No," he repeated.

She crushed the handkerchief in her hand. "What's the matter? What's happened to you? Why are you doing this?"

"It's got nothing to do with you, really," he said. "It's me, I suppose. I've changed."

The tears had dried. Now she raised her head and said, simply: "You're no traitor. You can't be. I don't believe it. Not you."

"Sorry."

She gasped, but tried to control herself. "Do you know what you're doing? Not just to me, but to your mother? You're killing her, do you understand? When they told her, she didn't believe them. She still can't. She lies there and waits for you to come through the door."

He bowed his head so that she would not see his agony.

"Please," she repeated, "it's not too late. Come home with me. For all our sakes."

"I can't," said Nicolai.

She gazed at him disbelievingly.

"Shura," he said in a low voice, "why did you inform on me?"

For a moment she seemed baffled. Then realization came. "I wanted to save you," she said.

"By telling them that I was going to defect? Why didn't you just shoot me?"

"You betrayed yourself, Nicky." She was suddenly in control of herself. "How much of a fool do you think I was? Every time you looked out of the window I knew what was in your mind. Every time you pretended to be asleep when I reached out for you, I knew what was going on. At first, I couldn't work it out. Then the odd word, the impatient gesture, the furtive look . . . oh, I knew, all right."

"So you ran to them. . . ."

"I was so confused. I couldn't understand why. Yes, I told Rostov. He's an old family friend, you know that. He's known me since I was this high. Yes, I told him." She was defiant now. "I hoped he could stop it. Save you for your country. Save you for me."

"You're a strange woman, Shura," he said quietly. "Your sense of loyalty is even stranger."

"Loyalty!" she cried out. "You're a fine one to talk."

He stood up. "That's it, then, isn't it?" He stared down at her. "It's finished, isn't it?"

But he thought: By the devil she's beautiful.

"No," she almost screamed, and jumped up. "Don't you understand, I love you? I hate what you've done, but I love you. Come back to me. . . ."

"Why don't you stay here with me?" he asked suddenly.

She stood very straight. Then she slowly started shaking her head. "I can't, you know I can't. What would happen to my father—in *his* position? And my brother? It would be the end for him. . . ." She had tears in her eyes. "No, you mustn't even ask me. Oh, don't you understand . . ." Now she was sobbing uncontrollably.

"I'm sorry, Shura," he said.

She embraced him again, and held him, her eyes closed. "I'll never see you again," she whispered.

"Don't say that."

"No, it's true," she sobbed. "I know it."

She tore herself out of his arms, and ran to the door. She stopped there and looked at him, her eyes still tear-filled. Then she rushed out the door, slamming it behind her.

He stood facing the bewhiskered old men in their gilt frames, but he didn't see them.

Spence came into the room.

"Well," he said, "I guess that's that."

"I want to get drunk," said Nicolai. "I want to get drunk out of my mind. Do you understand that?"

"I might even join you," said Spence.

Washington

"How is he getting on?" asked Gail.

"Why?" demanded Bishop. "What is it to you?"

He had been surprised when she asked to see him. He had made her wait, and when she was finally shown in, his manner was distant.

"He is my case," she said. "I want to know."

"No, Gail," corrected Bishop. "He *was* your case. You've done your part. It's got nothing to do with you anymore."

She crossed her legs and lit a cigarette. She was very self-possessed. "Where is he?" she asked.

"There is no need for you to know. I don't mean that unkindly, but you know the rules. He is being processed. He's well and safe. You needn't worry."

"I'd like to see him," said Gail.

Bishop's eyes narrowed. "Why?"

"I'd just like to," she said coolly.

"Sorry," he said. "You're out of it now."

She looked angry. "What's the problem?" she asked "He's not a prisoner, is he?"

The Admiral had been right, he thought. The old boy could be quite shrewd at times.

"Tell me, did you get involved with Galov?" he inquired abruptly. He saw her flinch, and corrected himself: "Or did he get involved with you?"

"Wasn't that the idea?" she said.

That comes of using amateurs, he thought regretfully. The well-heeled lady who wants to be a secret agent because she is bored with being a widow. Who pulls strings and gets taken on by the agency and then starts becoming entangled with the subject who's her target. It couldn't happen with a professional.

"Oh, I see," she said, as if she were reading his thoughts. "You don't approve. I've done my job, and I shouldn't care less about him now. That's the code. I'm being self-indulgent."

Bishop was starting to get angry. "Let me tell you some home truths about your Mr. Galov," he said harshly. "He's a calculating, cold-blooded son of a bitch. He's a KGB man who's done some very dirty things in a dirty outfit. He's only interested in Nicolai Galov. He's married, and has thrown his wife to the wolves. He had a mother, and he has abandoned her to the tender mercies of his late colleagues. He's not a very nice character, and don't let him fool you that he's anything but a bastard who's chosen to change sides because it suits him."

Her knowing smile annoyed him even more. "You really don't like him, do you?"

"I don't trust him." He decided to make it really tough for her. "And it's your duty not to trust him, either."

"That's your job, I guess," she said. "But I want to see him."

"No way," said Bishop.

"You can't keep him locked away forever."

"I can keep him until I've squeezed him dry," he said grimly.

She was anxious, that was clear. "But isn't he telling you everything you want to know? Hasn't he kept his side of the bargain? What else do you want from him?"

"He's come up with a lot of information, sure. He answers our questions. But it'll take us a long time to find out what those answers are really worth. Anyway, that's not your problem. Just keep out of it."

"Are you stopping me from seeing him?" she challenged.

"Yes," he said firmly.

"What are you afraid of?"

"I smell emotional involvement, and there's no room for that." He looked her straight in the eye. "I must say I'm surprised. Your husband was killed fighting these bastards. You said you wanted to do this work to help repay them for that. Now this."

"You want me to quit?" she asked in a low voice.

"Don't you understand, I'm not interested in personalities. It's up to you how useful you can be. Get involved in relationships with the other side and you know what I have to do. Get rid of you."

"Get rid of me?" she repeated.

He gestured impatiently. "Oh, for Pete's sake. You know what I mean. Separate you from the agency for the good of the service. Ask you to resign. Maybe that would be best for everybody. . . ."

"But I still couldn't see him, not even then?"

"That's right," said Bishop.

"But if I'm out of it, how can you stop me."

"I can stop you, Gail, believe me," he said brutally.

She nodded, and he was surprised at her sudden acquiescence. He had half expected an outburst, but all she said was: "I see."

"You want some advice, Gail?" His tone was kinder. "Forget about the guy. He was an episode. He's not worth it."

"Thank you," she said tonelessly.

"It's in everybody's interest."

"Is it?" she asked.

After she had gone, Bishop called in his secretary and dictated an urgent top-secret interoffice memo to personnel.

It asked that Mrs. Gail Howard's security clearance be immediately reviewed and insisted that from this date she was not to have sight of or access to any of the department's classified information or documents.

Safe House

NICOLAI VIKTOR GALOV

Transcript of Debriefing
No. 27

Interrogator: Robert Spence
Time: 10:41 A.M.

Q: Let me show you a photograph. Do you know this man?

GALOV: No.

Q: Does the name Bogdan Karlovski strike a chord?

GALOV: No. No, I don't think so. Is he the man?

Q: Yes. How about Peter Klass?

GALOV: Should that mean something to me?

Q: He was one of your illegals. In Switzerland. In the late '60s.

GALOV: Before my time.

Q: He defected to us in 1969,

GALOV: Oh, did he?

Q: How about Rudolf Gabrilovich?

GALOV: Who is he?

Q: Just think.

GALOV: Gabrilovich? I don't . . . oh, wait a moment. Wasn't he . . . oh, yes, I remember him.

Q: Tell me.

GALOV: They had to change the diplomatic ciphers after he absconded. He stole the ciphers used by our embassies in Stockholm and Oslo. And Helsinki. I think. In '70.

Q: April '71. That's right. Does the name Joe Silkin tie in?

GALOV: Who's he?

Q: Never mind. Have you heard of a man called Kravisky? . . . Why do you shake your head?

GALOV: Because it means nothing to me.

Q: This is his picture.

GALOV: No, I have never seen him.

Q: And I don't suppose the name Jake Brown is familiar to you?

GALOV: Why should I know him? What are you trying to find out?

Q: Bear with me, Nick. Try this photo.
Silence.

Q: Well?

GALOV: That is Feliks Tarasov.

Q: Ah. Tell me what you know.

GALOV: He is listed as a deserter. A traitor. He has been circulated to all our Referenturas. He was one of our key men in Warsaw. You know all that. It was to you that he went over.

Q: You don't link the name Felix Thompson with him?

GALOV: No.

Q: You sure?

GALOV: Of course. Why Thompson?

Q: Would you like a drink?

GALOV: Not now. What's the point of all this? What have these men to do with me?

Q: All colleagues of yours, isn't that right?

GALOV: Some of the names I have heard, yes. Tarasov. Gabrilovich. Not the others. And I've never met any of them.

Q: I ask you again. Quite sure?

GALOV: We are a very big organization, we have many sections, and many, many people. It's not very strange. Do you know everybody in your service?

Q: Have you heard them discussed, these names I gave you?

GALOV: In our service, traitors are never discussed. It is taboo. Far better to forget about it. A wise man does not mention the unmentionable.

Q: You said Tarasov was on a death list. . . .

GALOV: I did not say death list.

Q: Come along, Nick. You said he had been circulated to all your field stations. It's the same thing, isn't it? Anyway, what about the others?

GALOV: I suppose they too, of course, if they have betrayed their trust. I take it they have all defected over here?

Q:	That's right.
GALOV:	I guess I may even yet meet some of them, eh?
Q:	No. You won't.
GALOV:	Why not? We must be a very exclusive club.
Q:	Are you afraid at all, Nick?
GALOV:	Afraid of what?
Q:	Well, I imagine you realize you've been put on that list now?
GALOV:	Of course.
Q:	Does it worry you?
GALOV:	I rely on you and your superiors and the United States Government to protect me.
Q:	So you're not worried?
GALOV:	What exactly are you trying to do? Make me nervous? Of course I know that if they get me, they will try to kill me. That is something I will have to live with for the rest of my life. All defectors do. But I am sure you will take good care of me.
Q:	We'll do everything we can, you know that.
GALOV:	I am confident.
Q:	Good. This may sound naïve, but I'm interested to hear your answer. Why is the KGB so anxious to kill defectors?
GALOV:	I'm surprised you even ask. Obviously to punish traitors.
Q:	Is that the only reason?
GALOV:	To discourage anyone else from playing the same game. That, of course, is the other reason.
Q:	But it didn't discourage you?
GALOV:	My dear friend, I've been playing a dangerous game for a long time. I don't intend stopping now.
Q:	Oh. You are still playing it?
GALOV:	A figure of speech, that's all. Could I have that drink now?
Q:	Sure.

Interrogation ended: 10:59 A.M.

The Watch Room

Spence stood beside Dr. Harmer in the dimly lit surveillance chamber, watching the screens monitoring Nicolai's room.

"That's what I wanted you to see, Doc," he said. "Just look at him. Pacing up and down, up and down. Like a caged tiger."

"Maybe that's what he is," murmured Harmer. "How long has he been like this?"

"He's gotten very restless in the last twenty-four hours," said Spence. "I guess it's getting on his nerves, the questioning, the watching."

"Nothing strange about that."

"He said he wasn't having enough exercise. He's started jogging around the grounds in the morning. . . ."

"Alone?"

"He's never alone, Doc, even when he thinks he is." Harmer had to smile at the quiet pride with which Spence said it.

"That's probably one of the things that's getting him down."

"I think you'd better talk to Sergeant Lindner," said Spence. "This way, Doc."

"Who is Lindner?" asked Harmer.

"One of the marine guards."

The sergeant was a broad-shouldered, thick-set recruiting-poster image of a leatherneck, with a formidable row of campaign ribbons.

"Tell Dr. Harmer what you said in your report," Spence instructed.

The sergeant eyed Harmer a little cautiously. The marines, all of them handpicked, knew they were responsible for the security of a highly secret place. They had gotten used to the mysterious people who were kept there, and the anonymous spooks who came and left, sometimes in the middle of the night, in their black government cars. But they had made a point of keeping their distance from all of them.

"Go on, Sergeant Lindner," said Harmer encouragingly.

"Well, sir," said the sergeant, "I thought I ought to report it. It probably doesn't mean a darn thing, but I guess you never know."

"Absolutely," said Spence.

"When the Russki goes jogging, we keep an eye on him, of course, like we always do. Well, yesterday I lost sight of him for a little while, and then I found him, standing still."

"Yes?" said Harmer.

"He was standing still at the bottom of the security wall, behind the trees, and I got the feeling he was kind of reconnoitering it."

"You mean, you thought he was working out whether he could get over it?"

"That's it, sir. So I figured I'd give him a little warning. I told him that there were all kinds of wires and alarms on that wall, and that anybody who tried to climb it would find himself caught in thirty seconds."

"And what did he say, Sergeant?" asked Harmer.

" 'That's very reassuring.' But it didn't sound right."

"What happened then?"

"Well, sir, he looked at my ribbons and he said something about my having seen a lot of service. He asked me where I had been, and I said all over the place, you name it. He asked me if I had ever done duty at an embassy. I said, sure, I was with the London embassy, and in Athens. And I had been in the first shootout before the mob stormed the embassy in Teheran. Told him I was lucky to get transferred out just in time."

The sergeant paused, then resumed:

"Well, I suddenly got the feeling he was giving me a snow job, getting me to talk so that I'd forget what I'd seen. And then he suddenly said, 'Tell me, Sergeant, where are we? Where actually is this place?' "

"And you said . . ."

"I said, 'I'm sorry, sir, the location of this house and anything to do with it is classified and we have orders never to discuss it.' And he said, 'I'd hate you to violate your orders' and went jogging back to the main building. I thought about it and decided I should report it all."

"You did exactly right, Sergeant," said Spence.

"Thank you, sir."

After the marine had gone, Harmer lit his evil-smelling pipe. Spence dreaded even the sight of it.

"Interesting," said Harmer after a while, "but not un-expected."

"Do you think our friend is trying to get away?"

"Go over the wall, literally? No, I don't believe that. But I think you'd better watch it. He's on edge. He's becoming jumpy. He wants out of here. Can you blame him? Cooped up the way he is, and not even knowing where?"

"That's up to Bishop," said Spence. "He hid one guy away for two years."

"Why?"

"He didn't trust him."

"And was he right?"

"Oh yes," said Spence. "Very much so."

"What about Galov?"

"Why don't you ask Bishop?"

"Well," said Harmer, "as long as he realizes the fuse is beginning to burn short . . ."

Washington

The Admiral had had a bad day. What was supposed to have been a briefing of a Senate committee by him had turned into a grueling inquisition of him by them.

Somehow he had gotten on the wrong side of the group, and unexpectedly they started firing at him all kinds of sniping shots. There were expressions used like "lack of information" and "failure of intelligence" and echoes of past disasters.

The Admiral had to sit there and squirm, and trot out the standby phrases.

"I'm afraid this is a very sensitive issue, which I cannot discuss now. . . ."

"We are entering an area involving highly delicate questions. . . ."

"I would jeopardize the efforts of several agencies if I went into this subject any deeper. . . ."

It didn't go down well with the committee and he knew it.

"I am sorry I cannot speak about this matter more frankly," he told one senator, who promptly retorted: "So am I."

After four hours, the committee adjourned and the Admiral strode to his car, grim-faced. He knew he had made a bad impression, that it would be fed to the media, that the White House would sit up and take notice and talk to him reprimandingly.

"Back to the office, sir?" asked his driver.

"Yes," said the Admiral. He reflected bitterly that other countries' spymasters had a much easier life. Take that suave Englishman with the carnation in his buttonhole who was Director General of MI5. By law, they wouldn't even be allowed to identify him in the newspapers. The outfit didn't exist on paper, and they couldn't even ask questions about it in Parliament. Or Andropov and the rest of the KGB chieftains. Imagine them having to worry about public opinion, or being grilled by some vote-seeking legislator from the Corn Belt.

When he got back to his office, his secretary saw his mood written on his face like a road sign.

"You have only one appointment," she said soothingly. "Mr. Bishop."

He felt like saying, "What the hell does he want?" but instead he nodded.

"Let's have him in if he's ready."

Bishop sensed the atmosphere, too. Especially when the Admiral greeted him with a question:

"What good news do you bring me, Carl?"

"It's Galov, Admiral."

"Yes," nodded the Admiral grimly. "I've been wondering when you'd have something for me. Well?"

"I don't trust the man."

"Why don't you?"

"I can't say. Just a feeling. Everything fits and yet it doesn't."

"Are you trying to say that he is a double agent?" the Admiral asked impatiently.

"Not in so many words. . . ."

"Damnit, Carl, either he is or he isn't. Have you got evidence? Have your people picked up something?"

"No," said Bishop.

"Then what is it?"

"Instinct."

"I'm not in the guessing-game business," said the Admiral. It still rankled to recall one of the senators saying the agency was making too many guesses, most of them the wrong ones. "I am interested in facts. Produce solid evidence, and I'll accept it."

"Admiral, I can make out a good case against myself. He's given us a lot of valuable in-depth information. Nothing sensational, but very useful background material that only a man in his position knows about. He's answered the questions pretty openly. He's shown willingness."

"So what's wrong?" the Admiral demanded irritably.

"Nothing, I guess." But Bishop looked unhappy.

"If it's in your mind to hand him back, forget it."

"No, I wouldn't want that," said Bishop.

"Good, because it's out of the question. Anyway, is that all you have to tell me?"

"No, sir."

"What is it, then?"

Bishop hesitated only fractionally. "I want your authority, sir."

Suddenly the Admiral was interested. Bishop didn't often ask for special permission. Only when they entered dangerous ground.

"For what, Carl?"

"Galov, of course. I want to set him up."

"You know what you're saying?"

"Of course."

"They don't like us doing such things these days," the Admiral said with a sigh.

"It'll stay off the record."

"I don't think I want to know any more," the Admiral said hastily.

"Of course not. Thank you, Admiral."

"Carl."

"Sir?"

"Have you thought that you might be making a terrible mistake? That you're putting on the line the life of a man who's fled to us, who trusts us?"

"Very possibly."

"If things go wrong, you realize what you will have done?"

"Yes." Bishop's face was hard.

The Admiral looked away. "All right," he said. "Go ahead."

Safe House

NICOLAI VIKTOR GALOV

Transcript of Debriefing
No. 31

Interrogator: Carl Bishop
Time: 17:03

Q: You have something you want to tell me?

GALOV: Those men I was asked about the other day. Tarasov and the rest.

Q: Yes?

GALOV: They all defected to the United States?

Q: As you know.

GALOV: Why did you ask me about those four. I mean, there have been scores of defectors. Why ask me about these specific men?

Q: We are interested to know if you can help us about them.

GALOV: Help you, how? I don't even know them. What have I to do with these four?

Q: They all died. Very recently.

GALOV: All four?

Q: They were murdered. By the KGB, over here. Didn't you know?

GALOV: Of course not.

Q: Nick, I think you know more than that. One of your duties was liaison with Department V. The executive action department, right? "Direct activities," isn't that the phrase? Assassinations, for example.

GALOV: Yes.

Q: Speak up. Your voice is very low. This is being recorded, and the machine must pick you up.

GALOV: I'm sorry. Yes, I understand. It must be Dnieper. I hadn't realized they were actually implementing it. . . .

Q: What is this Dnieper?

GALOV: A special operation. They'd been talking about it a long time. But I didn't know it had started.

Q: What is this operation?

GALOV: Very simple. To eliminate former defectors who are secreted away under false identities.

Q: Even if they are no longer of value to anybody?

GALOV: That doesn't matter. The object is to discourage future defectors. After all, who is going to entrust his life to the United States authorities if they appear unable to safeguard him, even with false names and all the rest of it? If the flow of defectors can be cut off, you lose your most valuable source of secret information.

Q: Tell me more.

GALOV: Of course, when Department V first proposed it, there was one big snag. That's what held it up.

Q: What snag?

GALOV: Would you please lower that lamp. It is hurting my eyes.

Q: Sorry. Is that better?

GALOV: Yes. Thank you.

Q: What was this snag you mentioned?

GALOV: Well, obviously the key factor of Dnieper is to find these hidden defectors in their new surroundings. To track them down, wherever they are.

Q: So you had to find somebody who has the list.

GALOV: That proved impossible. Department V tried, but it turned out to be quite impossible.

Q: So what was the next step?

GALOV: Dnieper was held in abeyance. Put on ice, as you would say. Until somebody had a brilliant idea.

Q: What was that?

        Pause.

Q: Why are you holding up your hands like that?

GALOV: What was the first step in my debriefing?

Q: You had a medical.

GALOV: And the next?

Q: We started interrogation sessions.

GALOV: No. You took my fingerprints.

Q: And?

GALOV: That was it. Fingerprints. What happens to every alien who is registered in this country? And to every defector who is given sanctuary? You take his fingerprints.

Q: Don't stop.

GALOV: That's what Department V realized. Your people can change a defector's identity, give him a new name, alter his appearance, dye his hair, make him so different his own mother wouldn't recognize him. The one, the only thing that never changes are his fingerprints.

Q: But how . . .

GALOV: Once they realized that, the only problem that remained was to infiltrate somehow into the department that has all fingerprints on file. Our headquarters of course had the prints of all the defectors. So it just became a question of tracing the same prints in the American archives. Those archives would have the names, the new identities, the new whereabouts. . . .

Q: Why didn't you tell us this sooner?

GALOV: There were so many other things, other questions you wanted answered. . . .

Q: How did they get to the archives?

GALOV: Ah, that's why I didn't know that Dnieper had been activated. They were working on the fingerprint angle, trying to get a foothold, but I was out of it by then. I didn't really think they'd succeed, frankly.

Q: And you say this Operation Dnieper is now underway?

GALOV: Obviously. Whenever they want to make a hit, that is the word. They produce a set of fingerprints and ask their contact to trace it in your government files. If he locates them, they've traced another defector. I believe your fingerprint records are marvelously computerized. Two hundred million sets of prints, and you trace a single one in a couple of minutes. Department V must be very envious.

Q: All this is very helpful. Thank you.

GALOV: Good. But please don't forget to keep my own fingerprints under separate lock and key, do you mind?

Q: Don't worry. We've wrapped you in cotton wool. Interrogation ended: 17:28.

Washington

Bishop opened the combination lock on his smart leather briefcase and took out a thin folder with the highest security classification.

"Read this," he said to the deputy director of the FBI.

It was late at night, but what he had told the deputy director over a secure phone line was enough for him to stay on in the FBI headquarters building to await Bishop's arrival.

"What is this?" asked the deputy director.

"It's the transcript of an interrogation this evening," said Bishop. "With our defector."

"The KGB man?"

Bishop nodded. "You won't like it. Those killings that have been driving us crazy—seems the leak is right here."

"I don't believe it," said the deputy director. In the tradition of his bureau, he had no warm feelings toward Bishop and his agency. Least of all when they burst in on him with this kind of thing.

"Read it," Bishop repeated grimly.

He watched the face of the deputy director, but it betrayed nothing as he quickly scanned the typewritten pages.

"You believe this?" the deputy director said finally, putting the sheets down.

"It makes sense, every word of it," said Bishop. He was about to add "whether you like it or not," but he decided to forebear. He needed their cooperation, after all.

"The Bureau of Identification has some two thousand employees, but each one is screened and security-cleared," said the deputy director, rather defensively.

"Do you want me to give you the list of Soviet spies over the years who have been screened and security-cleared?" Bishop was getting impatient. "I know it hurts to think that even one is a traitor, but we've got to find him."

"What do you want me to do?" asked the deputy director.

"I want an all-out internal investigation mounted tonight. I imagine the way it works, when somebody wants a fingerprint traced, he sends through a requisition or something. The way somebody in a public library wants to see the books under a catalogue heading?"

"Something like that."

"You must go through the recent tracer slips with a fine-tooth comb," ordered Bishop. "We've got to find the guy who asked for the prints of our four defectors."

"They wouldn't even be listed under their names," said the deputy director. He tried to stop himself resenting the way this guy was telling him how the job should be done.

"Of course not." Bishop looked at him almost pityingly. "You don't imagine we'd let anybody have those. No, they'd be under their new names. Joe Silkin. Peter Klass. Felix Thompson. Jake Brown. Hell, you got the list."

"I've had fifty agents working on those killings," the deputy director said reproachfully. "Working all out."

"Yeah, and the clue's under your own roof," replied Bishop unkindly.

"It's going to be a dead end," insisted the deputy director.

Bishop looked at his watch. "We're wasting time," he said.

The deputy director reached for his phone.

Ossining

It felt strange. At last he was on his own, able to walk out of the front door, to do, apparently, as he liked. He was now called Roger Nicholls. Nicolai wondered why they had chosen that name for him; he did not feel like a Roger Nicholls.

He had a bank account, into which they had paid $5,000. They had promised him $500 a month. His new home was a cottage on a small street in Ossining, only a short walk from the gaunt walls of Sing Sing prison.

They told him that twice a week a woman would come in to clean the place. He had a telephone, but the number was unlisted.

"Take your time to get adjusted," they instructed him. "Find your bearings. Think what you'd like to do. Then we'll have another talk. We'll help you to set yourself up."

He had smiled at the phrase, but Spence's face had looked quite innocent.

"If you have any problem, anything bothers you, anything suspicious happens, call this number, day or night. Somebody will always be available to help you."

"Can I have a gun?" asked Nicolai.

"You think you need one?"

"Well, I'd feel a lot safer. Help can take a long time to come."

"Oh, don't worry about that," Spence had said reassuringly. "But we'll think about that. A gun permit won't be any trouble."

"And what about a passport?"

"What do you need that for?" said Spence. "You're not going anyplace. Are you?"

"You took my old one. And now I can't move anywhere."

"If ever you need to travel, you'll be taken care of," replied Spence, and again Nicolai was amused at the unwitting choice of words.

Spence looked around the cottage. It was pleasantly furnished in an old-fashioned sort of style, chintz curtains, neocolonial furniture, a small brick fireplace. A biggish back garden. Two bedrooms.

"*Two* bedrooms?" Nicolai had noted.

"Well, could be useful. If somebody has to stay here overnight." Spence nodded approvingly as he tested one of the beds. "You'll be comfortable, all right."

"Who are my neighbors?" asked Nicolai.

"They're perfectly all right," said Spence. "The guy next door works for the Department of Corrections. Nice family. And No. 32 is a doctor at the jail."

"Is there anybody who doesn't work for prisons around here?"

"Well, it *is* Ossining," said Spence. They walked into the kitchen. "Can you cook, Nick?"

"Eggs and bacon, and anything in a can."

Spence threw open a cupboard door. Its shelves were stacked with tinned food. The refrigerator was loaded.

"You won't starve, you see. And there's a very good Italian eating place, ten minutes around the corner."

"What about a car?"

"A car?" repeated Spence blankly.

"How do I get about?"

"Don't think you need a car right now," said Spence. "It's a small place, everything's in the neighborhood. What do you need a car for?"

"Supposing I want to go somewhere? To New York, say?"

"Listen, old buddy, it's best if you don't go too far afield for the time being," replied Spence earnestly. "You'll be secure here. You can go for walks, to the movies, shopping. Nobody knows who you are, and that's fine, but there's no point in taking chances, is there? It won't be for long, and then you make some trips. But not now, okay?"

After that they had a drink—there was a well-stocked liquor cabinet—and Spence told him to call that number if he needed anything, or had a problem. "Day or night, Nick, day or night."

"Some of the boys may drop by, just in case you get too lonely," he added vaguely. "But I guess you'll enjoy being away from all our faces and the questions and all that."

He was right too, thought Nicolai, after he had gone. Obviously they'd keep an eye on him, from a distance. The phone was probably tapped. But, curiously, try as he could, he found no signs of surveillance. He searched the cottage very thoroughly, spent three hours examining nooks and crannies, furniture, floorboards, ceiling light fixtures, but he drew a blank. If they had installed electronic ears, he couldn't find them.

In the afternoon, he went for a walk, looked across the gray Hudson River, and at the forbidding exterior of the penitentiary. He ordered spaghetti and meatballs at the Italian restaurant Spence had recommended. They had given him a whole wardrobe in the safe house before he left, and he looked very American.

He was obsessed with the notion that somebody was shadowing him, but gradually he relaxed. There wasn't anybody. They had left him off the leash, as far as he could see.

Before he left the safe house, they had asked him what plans he had for the future.

"I don't care, as long as I get away from this business," he said.

"What business?" they had asked.

"This. Spooks. Spies. Intrigue. Espionage. Security. Intelligence. The whole damn bag of dirty tricks. I'm through. I don't mind what I do as long as I'm out of that."

"Well," they had said, after a pause, "we'll help you

find just what you want. We'll finance you until you settle down. What kind of job were you thinking of?"

"I don't know yet," he had replied. "I'll try to think of something."

"Fine," they had ended it. "We'll talk again when you've come up with a proposition."

He came back from his first walk, and he found he was whistling. It surprised him. It was something he hadn't done for years. To his astonishment, he found he was relaxed. He decided it must be the absence of armed guards with their walkie-talkies, the probing cameras, the fact that he could make himself a cup of coffee, sit down, and switch on the TV without an observer noting the time and his demeanor.

It was warm in the little cottage, and he was comfortable in the armchair with its flowered covers. He started to doze.

He didn't know how long it was before he heard a car pull up outside, and a door being opened and shut. Suddenly the coziness had gone. He was wide awake, tense.

There was a knock on the front door. He hesitated. Then came the second knock. Gentle but insistent.

He looked out of the window. Outside stood a red sports car. The knock came a third time.

Nicolai hesitated, then, warily, he opened the door, keeping it on the chain.

"Aren't you going to let me in, Nick?" said Gail.

Washington

The girl was sitting at her desk in the big, spacious office in which dozens of other people were also working behind desks, going through stacks of card files.

She was not attractive. She had a large nose, which overshadowed her plain face; only her hair was beautiful. She tried hard to make herself good-looking, called to her aid cosmetics and nice clothes. But she could not disguise the sad truth that men would rather not look at her.

She was stuffing a file card with a set of ten fingerprints back into the official registry envelope when the three men walked up to her desk.

"Miss Phillips? Lois Phillips?" asked one of them.

The girl looked up, surprised. The three men did not

have the usual plastic badge all visitors had to wear in this normally restricted floor.

"FBI," said the man. "We'd like to talk to you?"

She looked stunned. "Why?" she gasped. The envelope had slipped out of her hand and onto the desk, where there was a stack of others.

"Let's go to your supervisor's office," said the man. He and his two colleagues waited politely as she collected herself. "You lead the way," he said.

Mr. Oxley, her departmental supervisor, looked flushed when they came in.

"Sit down, Lois," he said uneasily. She sank into a chair.

"These gentlemen are from the FBI," said Mr. Oxley. "They want to ask you some questions."

"FBI?" she said, wide-eyed. "I don't understand. What's this all about?"

Mr. Oxley, who had sat down behind his desk, had a distinctly unhappy expression on his face.

"My name is Cohan," said the FBI man. He indicated his two companions. "These are Special Agents Sylvester and Brownlow."

She had never heard the names. They simply didn't register. She was just staring at them, terrified.

"What do you want?" she asked finally.

"Lois, these agents are investigating some irregularities —er, alleged irregularities in your section," muttered Mr. Oxley. "I'm sure, uh, that it doesn't concern you—I mean, that you have a complete explanation . . ."

"Miss Phillips, we have reason to believe that you have been making unauthorized and illegal use of government files," broke in Cohan.

"Oh my God," she said.

"You have been passing classified information to another party in violation of federal law," he went on relentlessly.

"No," she cried, "no . . ." She gave Mr. Oxley a frantic look, but he stared at the wall.

"Would you like to tell us about it?" said Cohan, mildly. His two companions had their notebooks out.

"I don't know what you're talking about," she said. Her lips were trembling.

"Did you pass on details listed about the owners of certain fingerprints in the bureau's files?" asked Cohan.

She shook her head. She was trembling.

"Specifically details obtained from the files of Peter Klass, Felix Thompson, Joe S. Silkin, and Jake Brown?"

"I . . . I don't even know who they are," she whispered. She dabbed her long nose with a handkerchief as if she wanted to hide it.

"Why don't you make it easy for yourself, Miss Phillips," said the agent called Brownlow. It was the first time he had spoken.

She had started to sob.

"It's good advice," said Cohan. "You could face charges of espionage. . . ."

"Espionage! Me? That's ridiculous."

"Did you pass that information?" demanded Cohan.

She looked at all of them in turn, and she saw no help in their eyes.

"It isn't what you say at all." Her voice was small, helpless. "It's not espionage. That's crazy. It's only for a credit agency. To find some people who owe money. I've only done it to help Frankie."

"Who's Frankie?"

"My boyfriend," she said proudly, almost defiantly. Yes, suggested her tone, I know I'm no pinup, I know you think I look like a dog, but I've got my Frankie. *He* loves me.

"What's his full name?"

"Frankie Pohlman."

"How does he come into it?" asked Brownlow.

She was becoming more self-possessed now. "Well," she said, "Frankie works for this agency, see? His job is to bring in outstanding debts. He's had a hell of a time tracing some of them. He said it would be a big feather in his cap if he could nail at least some of the guys who've disappeared owing clients money. We got talking one night, and I said at the place where I work, right here, we trace people every day. I told him how we can identify a fingerprint just like that—" She snapped her fingers. "Well, one day he brought me a set of fingerprints. He said they belonged to a fellow who's absconded owing thousands. Maybe we got a listing for him. So I took the photostat he gave me, and put out a tracer. Sure enough, the guy was listed. In New York City. I gave Frankie the address. He was delighted."

She looked blissful at the memory.

"Soon after he told me that they'd found the guy, and

got their money, and he brought me another lot of dabs. I was doing it as a favor, see?"

She waited for their comment, but they said nothing.

"Well, this one was listed in California, I think. Or maybe Arizona. Out West. Frankie was on cloud nine. He'd gotten a raise, he said. His boss was over the moon. Thanks to Frankie, they had recovered thousands. That's it. I know maybe I shouldn't have done it, but it was only to help Frankie. And what's wrong with bringing a few bad eggs to book?"

Mr. Oxley was aghast. "How could you do this, Lois," he whimpered. "That's completely unauthorized, and you know it."

"Just a moment, sir," said Cohan. "Miss Phillips, what is the name of this outfit? This debt-collecting agency?"

"I don't know," she said. "You'll have to ask Frankie." She added earnestly: "But you see how stupid it is to talk about espionage. I wouldn't do such a thing. I'm a loyal citizen. You must know that. The bureau checked me out."

"Yes, miss," said Brownlow. "And we did it again. When we found that you had put through tracers for these four men."

"Tell me about Frankie," said Cohan. "How long have you known him?"

She actually blushed. "About six months. But we're—we're pretty close."

"I see," said Cohan impassively.

"I'm seeing him tonight," she said. "I can ask him anything you want. . . ."

"Where? What time?"

"At the Parakeet Bar. Downtown. At six. As soon as I'm through here."

"Thank you," said Cohan.

"I'll tell him about the trouble he's caused me. He'll be very sorry. And I won't do it again, I promise."

"You're right there, Miss Phillips," said Cohan. "But I'm afraid you won't be seeing Frankie tonight."

"Oh?" Panic was growing. "Why not?"

"Because you're under arrest, Miss Phillips."

"Arrest!" She was white-faced. "What for?"

"I told you. Espionage."

She never heard them reading her rights to her. She was sobbing too uncontrollably.

Ossining

Gail reached out from the bed for a cigarette; Nicolai, lying beside her, watched her lithe, sleek movements.

"You want one?" she asked. He shook his head, and she lit her cigarette.

She has a beautiful body, he thought.

"How did you find me?" he asked, making it sound, he hoped, casual.

"Connections," she said, vaguely. "An uncle on Capitol Hill helps."

"So much for security." His tone was a little acrid.

"There aren't many closed doors in Washington, if you have the right key."

He frowned. "That's reassuring, for a man in my situation."

"Oh, don't worry, they're very special connections." She blew out some smoke. "And it wasn't easy." She stretched herself languidly. "But it was worth it." She leaned over and kissed him. It was a gentle kiss. Passion was spent for the moment.

"You said they've fired you," he said.

She shrugged her naked shoulders.

"Why?" he insisted.

"Does it matter?" she asked.

"I want to know. Why did they kick you out."

"Us," she said. "That's why."

"But do you know what you're doing?" he asked gravely. "What you've gotten yourself into?"

"Nick," she said, "let's take an oath. Right now. Let's promise each other we won't ask any questions. We'll never talk about the past, all right? We're only interested in now. That's all that matters. Now. The present. The past is dead."

He reached out and stroked her face. "But what about the future?" he said gently. "Our future, my love?"

"Let's take that as it comes. My God, you Russians can be very morose. Look at yourself. Full of gloom." She laughed. "I'm beginning to think I shouldn't have come. Come on, stop being like a character out of *House of the Dead*."

"All right, you crazy woman. You show me how to live it up."

She crushed the cigarette in the glass ashtray, and embraced him, her lips on his mouth.

Later, when they were lazing around, Nicolai said: "Are you going to stay here?"

"Why not? I've got my things in the car."

"But what about them?" He looked anxious. "They'll find out. How will they feel about it?"

"Nicolai," she cried, "stop it. Who cares? What does it matter what they think? They fired me for what they said was an unprofessional relationship. I might as well have one, and enjoy it."

"Gail, is it safe?"

"You mean your old friends?"

"I don't know who I mean anymore," he said wearily. "When I heard your car I jumped. When you knocked, my pulse was going like a machine gun. I smell danger everywhere. And did you know that four defectors they were looking after have been killed?"

"Yes," she said quietly.

"You knew! And you didn't tell me?" He stared at her.

"Would you have, in my shoes?" she asked. She came close to him. "They sent me to bring you over here. To arrange for you to go through with it. At first—well, it was merely a job. I had my orders. Then I wanted you to come to us. I wanted you here. If I had told you the KGB had managed to find and kill four men we were sworn to protect, it might have made you . . . well, change your mind. Of course I didn't tell you."

"I see."

She put her arms on his shoulders and looked straight into his eyes. "Nick," she said, "stop it. We're not going to spend our time worrying. We're out of it, thank God. Let's have fun. Let's enjoy ourselves. Go out to dinner. Talk about clothes. Play games. Go to bed. Forget the rest, Mr. Roger Nicholls. You never knew Vice Consul Nicolai Galov. He's far, far away." She kissed him, hard.

When he released her, she saw herself in the mirror.

"Look at my lipstick!" she cried.

She grabbed her bag, and opened it, and it was then he saw the pistol nestling in it.

He reached for it, and took it out. It was a .38 service pistol. "What's this, Gail?" he asked quietly.

Her eyes dulled over. Then she forced a laugh. She held out her hand, and he gave the gun back slowly.

"This little thing?" she said with a false brightness. "Why, Nick, a girl has to take some precautions these days, doesn't she?"

She put the gun back, and started repainting her lips.

"Now," she said when she had finished, "what would you like for dinner?"

She put her handbag away, but he could not forget the gun.

Washington

Not many people saw the arrest. The man had been leaning against the bar, looking a couple of times at his watch. He was waiting for somebody, and the person was late.

He was a good-looking man, with wavy hair, a handsome face, smart clothes. He wore handmade shoes and a silk tie.

Three men approached him. He looked startled when they spoke to him, and then paid the bartender. He then left with the trio. Outside, at the curb, a black car was waiting. They held the door open for him. One of the men got in beside him in the back seat, and the other two got in the front. Then the car drove off.

"What the hell is this?" asked the wavy-haired man, his American tinged with a German accent.

"You're under arrest, Mr. Pohlman," Cohan announced.

"You must be kidding. What for?"

"You'll find out."

The car stopped at a traffic light.

"Where are you taking me?" demanded Pohlman. "I got a date. I was waiting for her."

"Don't worry. Lois won't be coming."

"What's that supposed to mean?" Pohlman said angrily.

"She's under arrest, too," said Cohan.

Pohlman had turned pale.

Two hours later, in a bare room, with a light shining on him so brightly that he blinked, he sat in a chair. No longer suave and self-controlled. He licked his lips, his hair was rumpled, and he looked around uneasily, like a trapped animal that knows its peril.

"Go on," prompted Bishop. Pohlman couldn't see his features, just a shadowy figure behind that glare.

"So I started dating her. That's all there is to it."

"You work for Lufthansa on Fifth Avenue. In Manhattan?" asked Cohan.

"That's right."

"And you live in Brooklyn?"

"Yes."

"Isn't it mighty inconvenient to date a girl who lives in Washington?"

"It's only an hour from LaGuardia," said Pohlman, a little desperately.

"Expensive, these dates, aren't they?" pressed Cohan. "And you're a sharp dresser, Mr. Pohlman. Those shoes, the tie, they cost money. You get paid that well as a reservations clerk?"

Pohlman swallowed. "I . . . I make a little on the side."

"Sure you do," said Cohan amiably. "For special services. I wonder for whom?"

"I don't get you."

"Try this," said Bishop. "According to immigration, you came to this country two years ago. You're a German national. Hometown Berlin. But to get there, you crossed the wall. You come from Stettin."

"Yes," croaked Pohlman.

"That's East Germany."

Pohlman gripped the arms of his chair. His tie was loose and he was perspiring. "That's why I left," he cried, "why do you think I risked my neck going over the wall?"

He didn't look so handsome now, in the state he was in, but he was still a good-looking man. She must have been swept off her feet, poor little Lois, thought Bishop. This pinup guy with his wavy hair and handsome face making a play for her. Little Miss Plainface being wooed by this charmer.

"I'm more interested to know who the man is for whom you do these special services," said Bishop.

They broke off the interrogation twice. The room was thick with tobacco smoke, and cups of coffee were strewn all over. But apart from the two breaks, they kept at Pohlman from all sides. questioning, never letting go.

At 4:32 A.M. Pohlman broke.

"He came to me," he gasped, gray-faced. "He said he

had greetings from my parents. In Stettin. In East Germany. He said they were well, and sent me their love. He said he wanted me to do a little job. It would pay well."

"Where was this?"

"He came up to me in Rockefeller Center one lunchtime. He was very friendly. But then he changed his tune. He said if I didn't do what he asked, there might be trouble for my parents. Black-market charges. Economic sabotage. Anything. I understood."

"He gave you photostats of fingerprints?"

Pohlman nodded wearily. "One set at a time. He told me to make friends with a girl clerk who works in the fingerprint department at the FBI. He said it would not be too difficult. They've got hundreds of little-girl clerks, and at noon they're all over the place, at lunch counters, sunning themselves. It shouldn't be difficult to pick one up." He lowered his head. "It wasn't," he said.

"Did he tell you why they wanted the identities of these fingerprints?"

"No, not really. He said something about them being criminals on the run, and the Americans weren't being helpful. He wasn't very clear." He rubbed his nose. "He paid a thousand dollars a shot, and five hundred a week expenses."

"Ah," said Bishop. "Generous." He emerged from behind the glare. "Is this your pal, Frank?" he asked. He held out the photo-fit composite of the man in steel-rimmed glasses. "Do you recognize him?"

Pohlman's bloodshot eyes squinted at the picture. "I—I think so. It's almost like him. Yes, I think it's him." He looked up. "How do you know?"

"Never mind. What's his name?"

Pohlman shook his head. "No." He licked his lips again. "No, I can't. I daren't."

"You'd better tell us," warned Cohan.

"Don't you see," cried Pohlman. "What will happen . . . to my parents . . ."

"I'll tell you what will happen to you," snarled Cohan. "You'll never leave jail alive. They'll put you inside for ninety-nine years. They'll throw the key away, that I promise."

They waited.

"Well, how about it?" said Bishop gently.

"Nobody will know . . . that I . . . you promise?"

"Nobody will know, ever," Bishop assured him smoothly.

"All I know is he calls himself Mr. Skinner. That's all, honest."

"How do you two communicate?"

"He takes me to lunch. A different place each time. We fix up the next place every time we meet."

"You say you can't contact him?"

"He's never given me a phone number or anything," said Pohlman. "That's the truth."

"All right." Bishop pulled up a chair and sat close to him. "When's the next get-together?"

"Day after tomorrow."

"Where?"

"In New York. Gallagher's Steak House."

"What time?"

"Noon."

Bishop tapped the photo-fit picture. "And that's how he looks?"

"Yes, yes. I told you."

"What's supposed to happen?"

Pohlman gulped. "He gives me my money. And any instructions . . ."

"A new set of fingerprints?"

"Maybe." He looked at Bishop pleadingly. "What's going to happen to me?"

Then he wept.

New York

Igor Valerian liked to eat liver. Before he arrived at the restaurant he had already decided that he was going to have the liver steak. Gallagher's did it to perfection. He would enjoy it, even if he wouldn't enjoy the company.

"I have a table," he told the maître d'. "The name is Skinner."

The man checked his register. Then he said: "Yes, Mr. Skinner. This way, please."

It was a nice table by the wall, beneath a row of photographs of boxers, and within sight of the bar in the center.

"Bring me a whiskey sour," ordered Valerian. "While I wait for my guest."

Whiskey sours were another taste he had acquired in

this country. When his recall came, he would miss some of these things.

The man in the gray suit sitting by himself at the next table but one studied him with more than passing interest. Bishop had recognized him immediately; it was uncanny how close the photo-fit had come to portraying Valerian. So this was the killer, the man who stalked the defectors. He didn't look sinister in the least, thought Bishop. Not that he had expected him to—but this man was unlike any KGB agent he had ever seen. More like a Madison Avenue ad executive.

Bishop had arrived half an hour early. One of his men had checked that Skinner had a reservation, and booked the nearest table for Bishop. Bishop smiled inwardly; it was going to be an interesting situation.

Valerian had his drink. He kept looking at the people coming in. Gradually he became annoyed. His thin lips pressed together disapprovingly.

"Waiter," he called out, "I'll have another whiskey sour."

It was 12:16. It was the third time he had checked his watch. He glanced around the restaurant as if to check that he and his lunch companion hadn't missed each other. His eyes swept over Bishop without pausing. There was no sudden alertness. He had no idea who Bishop was.

Bishop wondered what the man would do when Pohlman didn't show up. Wait. Or depart? Call somebody? Leave a message?

At 12:31, Valerian signaled the waiter. "Has there been a message for me?" he asked tersely. "Mr. Skinner?"

"I'll check, sir," said the Irish waiter. He was back quickly. "Nothing at all, Mr. Skinner."

"All right," said Valerian. "My guest must have been detained. I think I'll order."

Damn right, thought Bishop. You don't know how close you are. Your little contact is detained, very much so.

They ate side by side, with only the empty table between them. Valerian had his liver steak, but he wasn't fully enjoying it. He kept looking around, impatiently, like a lover who's been stood up. Bishop had a T-bone and enjoyed it enormously. It was turning into a very pleasant lunch, as far as he was concerned.

Again Valerian looked at his watch. It was 1 P.M. He had ordered coffee, and he sat, simmering. Then, after another quarter of an hour, he asked for his check.

Bishop didn't move. He was giving himself a treat, smoking a big, expensive cigar he had bought himself at the old tobacco shop on Madison Avenue. He watched Valerian pay his check in cash, saw him give one more searching look around the steak house, and at the men crowding the bar. Then Valerian, his face set grimly, walked out.

Bishop remained where he was, and asked for another coffee.

Outside, Valerian walked to Times Square and hailed a yellow cab. What he didn't know was that from the moment he had left Gallagher's, he was being followed by three shadows, spaced out strategically, and that the cab was being followed by a car in radio contact with the trackers.

The car followed the cab until it stopped at the UN Building. Valerian got out and walked in through the staff entrance, showing his ID card. He still wasn't aware that two men were on his tail, and that when they entered the UN Building they had identification that opens all doors. They were still with Valerian when he pushed the button in the elevator.

Washington

"His name is Igor Valerian. He is an administrative assistant with the Soviet delegation at the UN. He lives in the Russian complex on the East River. And he is our man." Bishop paused triumphantly.

"They're supposed to be under surveillance," said the Admiral. "How does he manage to get all over the place? California, Arizona, you name it. And we don't know anything about it?"

Bishop sighed. This was one of those times when the Admiral's naïveté was irritating.

"It's not difficult, sir," Bishop said patiently. "He looks American. He sounds American. He fits into the scenery. He grabs a cab, loses our tail, catches a flight he's booked under some other name, and is back in New York before anyone even knows he's been away. It's a free country. Cops don't ask you for identity cards."

The Admiral looked like a man with indigestion. "It's one hell of a mess, Carl," he said. "The State Department will hate it. If we arrest him, and tell the Soviets their delegation harbors a KGB killer agent, the Kremlin will raise the roof. You know they'll cut off their own nose for a little entente with Moscow. This could blow into something really nasty. They won't like us even uncovering it."

Bishop coughed politely. "Who said anything about arresting him?"

"Eh?"

"I'd like you to agree to us doing nothing."

"Leave this man at large? Damnit, he's killed four people already. He's breached our security wide open. No defector is safe while he's around."

"Exactly," said Bishop.

The Admiral, for once, was speechless. He was trying to find the right words, but Bishop didn't give him time.

"We'll be on his tail every second. If he sneezes, if he so much as spits, we'll know about it. But I want him to feel free."

"To do what?"

Bishop smiled.

Ossining

"You're drunk," said Gail.

"You're damn right I'm drunk," snapped Nicolai. He poured himself another drink. "And I'm going to get drunker." He gave a mirthless laugh. "Isn't that my democratic right?"

She looked at him, worried. "What's the matter, Nick? What's gotten into you? You haven't been yourself for days."

"Right again." He held out the bottle. "Want to join me?"

"What's wrong?" she repeated. She had put the bottle on the table. Out of his reach, she hoped.

"What can be wrong?" he said, and belched. "What can be wrong with a man nobody trusts?"

"Who doesn't trust you?" she asked quietly.

"You know damn well. They don't. Your pals. Commissar Bishop. Your KGB." He burped again. "Why did I ever bother? You tell me that? Why did I think that if I came over here, they'd understand. They'd understand that here is one Nicolai Galov, and all he wants is to be like Ferdinand. Sniffing the flowers in the field. Don't laugh." His voice was suddenly sharp. "It's not funny. It's not funny when a man realizes he is trapped. I thought once they dissected me, cut me into pieces, satisfied themselves, they'd let me be."

He took another drink.

"How wrong, my love. How wrong this stupid fool Galov was. I beg your pardon, this idiot Roger Nicholls. Poor, stupid Nicolai Roger damn Galov." He raised his glass, *"Prosit,* babushka."

"Nick, what's brought this on?" She was troubled.

"I am like a specimen. An animal in a cage." He waved his arms. "Sure, a nice cage. A pretty little cottage. Chintz curtains, even. Money paid into the bank. A beautiful woman to go to bed with at night." For a moment he paused. "A very beautiful woman, true. And I am as free as a man in the Lubyanka. The bed is softer, the food better."

She had become angry. "Is that all it means to you?"

"Oh, you mean I must be grateful. That I have been accepted with open arms, that they protect me. I am grateful. There. Shall I say it again? I am grateful." He looked up at the ceiling. "Do you hear that? I am very, very grateful."

"What do you want?" she demanded.

He put his fingers to his temples. "To be free in here. Not to have everything I do and say analyzed. Not to be 'that KGB man, that defector, that agent.' To be me."

"We are what we are, Nick."

"They won't let me be what I am." He reached for the bottle, but it was beyond his grasp. "Pass it over," he grunted. "Please."

"You've had enough, don't you think?" she said gently.

"You see?" he cried. "What did I say? Free! Who is free?"

Silently she pushed the bottle over to him.

"Thank you," he said. He filled his glass. "Maybe you do understand. I think you do." He nodded. "You are very beautiful in every way."

"Why do you say they don't trust you?"

He was silent for a moment. Then: "I know. I sense it. Yesterday I was walking but I did not feel alone. I brush my teeth, but I wonder who is there with me in the bathroom."

"You're imagining things."

"Tell me, is there something they are waiting for?"

"What do you mean?" asked Gail.

"Who knows? Perhaps they are waiting for somebody to contact me? Eh?"

"Who should contact you?" she frowned. "That's the last thing they want. You have to be hidden away for the present, don't you understand? In case they try to kill you . . ."

"Ah." He nodded to himself as if suddenly she had revealed a great truth. "That would prove I was genuine. If I were dead."

"Nobody doubts you're genuine."

"But of course they do," said Nicolai. "Once a traitor . . . If somebody killed me, they would know they misjudged me. But if nobody takes a shot at me, then I am suspect. Ironic, isn't it."

"That's nonsense," she protested.

He looked at her over the glass.

"Is it, my love?"

Washington

The headline was spanned the entire width of the front page: KGB DEFECTOR IN HIDING.

The story was exclusive and copyrighted:

A top KGB official who secretly defected to the United States is living in hiding in a small town in New York State.

Nicolai Viktor Galov, who was the Soviet Union's vice consul in Frankfurt-on-Main, West Germany, recently fled to this country, and after intensive debriefing by U.S. intelligence agencies, is now resident in Ossining, N.Y. He calls himself Roger Nicholls, and is living in strict seclusion.

Galov's diplomatic cover hid the fact that he was an officer of the KGB, working on secret assignments, and in charge of various illegal activities in Western Europe.

Since defecting, he has given much valuable information to the CIA, and provided leads that are now being followed up by U.S. intelligence.

One intelligence official described Galov's revelations

as "invaluable. He has given us the key to top-secret Russian activities. It is a breakthrough for us."

Galov's defection is so important that the KGB appealed, through Soviet diplomatic channels, to have him returned to Russia. The State Department bluntly rejected the request.

Galov is married, but his wife is now in Moscow.

Some of the information Galov has given about KGB operations is being passed by the United States to its NATO allies.

The Admiral almost threw the newspaper at Bishop.

"This is the biggest breach of security that has taken place since I took charge of this agency," he announced. "I'm going to see that the guy responsible is crucified."

"Well," said Bishop, "I guess you'll have to crucify me."

"I . . ." the Admiral began, and stopped. *"What* did you say?"

"I leaked the story," said Bishop. "They got it pretty accurate, don't you think?"

There was complete silence.

Finally the Admiral said, very quietly: "Have you gone insane, Carl?"

"I hope not, sir."

"You say you . . . *you* leaked this story?"

"Yes, Admiral."

A sharp intake of breath was the only sound from the Admiral.

"You deliberately blew this man's cover?" he finally asked.

"Yes, sir. If you want to put it that way . . ."

"What other way is there?" demanded the Admiral icily.

Bishop looked across at the window. "You gave me authority, sir," he said, almost as an aside. "You remember? I said I wanted to set him up. Well, I have."

"I gave you authority? To do this?" The Admiral had turned redder than Bishop had ever seen him.

"Goddamnit, man, you've signed his death warrant."

"I don't think so," said Bishop.

The Admiral grabbed the paper, and slapped it with his hand. "You give his cover name. You identify his whereabouts. You rub in salt by saying how he has been betraying secrets. He is a dead man, Bishop. Thanks to you."

He controlled himself.

"I'm going to give you a direct order, and you see it is carried out forthwith. Then I'm going to deal with you. But right now you get Galov out of there. Grab him as quick as you can. Find him a new hideout. And a new identity. Within the hour. And I hope we're not too late." He scowled at Bishop with intense dislike. "I should have gotten rid of you. When we weeded out the others. Get going."

Bishop sat in the chair.

"What are you waiting for, Mr. Bishop?"

"I think we should see what happens," said Bishop. "I really do."

"I'll tell you what will happen," said the Admiral through his teeth. "They're going to kill him, if they can get at him. Now they know where to find him. We've been going crazy trying to find how they traced those other defectors, and now you're doing the job for them." He snorted. "You know what the repercussions can be? Have you any idea what this is going to do to us, to the agency, to me?"

"It won't do you any harm at all, sir," said Bishop.

"What?"

"As far as the public is concerned, it's a great coup. You've pulled off a stroke. Got us a big catch, a real live KGB man with his bag of secrets. That's as far as the public is concerned. They'll say, terrific."

"Hmm. They won't say that, Carl, when the guy's assassinated under our noses because we couldn't keep our security watertight. Because you, damnit, babbled." The Admiral clenched his fist. "What the hell did you do it for?"

"If he's an open target, Admiral, they'll do one of two things. They'll either try to kill him, or they'll ignore him." Bishop's smile was not pleasant. "If they try to kill him, we know he's genuine. If they studiously avoid him even though they know where to find him—well, then we'd better think again about Mr. Galov."

The Admiral bit his lip. He decided that Bishop was definitely a dangerous man, devious as hell, calculating as the devil, but above all, dangerous.

"I'll take all the precautions, in case they do try a hit," added Bishop. "Of course."

"You've deliberately set him as a target," growled the

Admiral. "I can't allow that." His eyes narrowed. "Unless of course I don't know about it."

"Exactly, Admiral."

"You really don't trust him?"

"Let's say this is a safety test."

"A hell of a test." He chewed his lip again, a rare sign of uncertainty. "You sure you're thinking their way?" The Admiral was a brave man, often decorated for courage, but this was making him nervous.

"If Galov is what he says he is, a genuine defector, not a Trojan horse, they'll do anything, absolutely anything to shut him up and to pay him back for his treason. They have to. They can't let a KGB agent get away with it. If he is genuine."

"Suppose it goes wrong, and he is killed, and we've sacrificed a genuine defector who trusted us?"

Bishop looked straight into the Admiral's eyes. "Sir, it's very sad, but people die in war." He added, greatly daring, "And in detente."

"I don't talk politics," lied the Admiral. He stood up. "And I don't consider we've had this chat. But if you've made a mistake, I want your resignation. Within twelve hours."

"It's already typed, sir," said Bishop.

Ossining

"My God," said Gail. "Have you seen this?"

She handed him the newspaper.

"You've got to call Washington," she went on. "You must talk to Bishop."

He was still reading the story, expressionless.

"What was that?" he said remotely.

"They've got to get you away from here," she said, urgently. "Today. Now."

"What's the point?" He sounded tired. "They'll have seen it. They'll do what they want to . . ."

She picked up the paper again, scanned the story with disbelief. "I don't understand how this could have happened. How could it get out?"

"Didn't you see the by-line?" he asked wearily.

"Eddie Haze?" She shook her head. She sounded puzzled. "Do you know him. . . ?"

"Oh yes," said Nicolai. "I know him, all right. 'Washington bureau,' eh?" He shrugged. "He must have given up freelancing in Europe. I hadn't realized he was working here now."

"Who is he?" She was still clutching the paper.

"A journalist," said Nicolai. "Among other things. He made the first contact. With your Mr. Karstetter. I warned Bishop about him. . . ."

"I don't understand," said Gail. "Warned him about what?"

"That he might be playing a double game. After that day in Rudesheim, I had my doubts. . . ."

She put the paper down. "What are we going to do?"

"Nothing," he replied calmly. "There is nothing we can do. If they want to move me somewhere, they will. If not . . ."

"Don't be so bloody calm about it," she cried. "You're a sitting target now, don't you realize? They know where you are, they know what you're called. . . ."

He tried to joke about it. "I never did like the name Roger Nicholls."

"Well, if you're not going to do something about it I am." She jumped up.

"No," he said firmly. "You mustn't."

"I don't understand," she cried. "It's your life that's on the line. How can you take it so calmly."

"I've got to stop running. What's the use, anyway? I'm tired, Gail." He saw her face. "Look, they'll do their best to guard me. Leave it to them. What will be will be."

"You're not even fighting back anymore," she accused him bitterly.

"If there's one thing I was always taught, it is to be a realist." He helped himself to a cigarette. "We'll just be careful."

"You know what's going to happen. Hordes of newsmen. TV. Interviews. It'll be like a circus. . . ."

"I think Bishop and his friends may discourage that."

"In a free society you can't discourage the media. That's something you've got to learn, Nick."

"Gail," he said patiently. "It's you who may have to learn. When it comes to Bishop and his people, you'd be surprised what they can do."

Once more she picked up the paper, and looked at it as if the whole bad-dream front page might have changed. But the headline was still there. And the story splashed beneath it.

"How could this happen?" she said. "How could they let it?"

"Ask Mr. Haze sometime," said Nicolai.

"How can a newspaper even print it? They must know they're putting your life in danger." She was outraged now. "What kind of journalism is it, to risk a man's life for a story?"

"It is a very good story," said Nicolai. "Any reporter would give their right hand to get that scoop. I guess Mr. Haze is made."

They didn't talk much about it after that. Gail looked out of the windows several times, and he knew she was looking for—for what? The car standing watch? The plainclothes sentinels? Or the others? A suspicious figure lurking? A suspect couple across the street?

But no one appeared.

"Learn to live with it," said Nicolai. "You'll get used to it."

"I don't want you killed, Nick," she said simply.

"Don't worry, my love. I don't intend to be."

New York

Igor Valerian read the story, too.

Other things had been on his mind. Pohlman had apparently disappeared. He had vanished into thin air, and Valerian did not believe people did that without a very good reason.

He couldn't believe Pohlman had gone on the run. He wasn't the type. He was too yellow. He'd be scared of his own shadow. So what had happened to him?

Maybe he had been run over. Many people had accidents in New York City. Or somebody had mugged him. The guy wasn't important. He probably wouldn't even rate the papers unless the manner of the violence that had overtaken him was spectacular.

It was a possibility, a distinct possibility. But it still left Valerian vaguely uneasy.

He took a walk along Fifth Avenue and stared through the windows of the Lufthansa office. He couldn't spot Pohlman.

He went into the airline's office. He toyed with the idea of actually asking for Pohlman and then decided it wasn't wise. So he made an excuse to the girl who was about to ask him his business, and left.

It was worrying.

But all that was swept from his mind when he saw the story about Nicolai Galov, defector.

It was most interesting. Fancy, the Americans let newspapers get away with murder. Watergate had really been most useful. Ever since then, the KGB had been getting marvelous little tidbits just by reading what they called, what was the word, investigative journalism.

Valerian felt like writing this Eddie Haze and his editor a letter of thanks.

He cut out the story carefully. It would be useful when the exact orders came.

Ossining

Gail was making breakfast when the knock on the door came.

"I'll get it," said Nicolai.

"Wait," she ordered sharply. She rushed to her bag, and took out the .38.

"Don't be silly," said Nicolai. He looked out of the window. "It's only the mailman." He started toward the door, but she hissed:

"Don't you dare show your face."

He stopped. She went and cautiously opened the front door, keeping the chain on. She held the gun concealed.

"Package for Mr. Nicholls," said the mailman.

"Oh." She put the gun down. "All right." She opened the door cautiously.

"Good morning," said the mailman cheerfully. He handed a small square package to her. It was wrapped in brown paper and sealed with Scotch tape.

"Thank you," said Gail. She shut the door quickly, put back the chain.

"Be careful," said Nicolai.

She looked at the cancellation mark. "Local," she said. "Mailed right here in Ossining."

She went into the kitchen, came back with a pair of big scissors.

"I wouldn't touch it," said Nicolai.

She hesitated.

"Nobody is going to send me any little gifts," he said.

"You want me to call the bomb squad?" she asked, half serious, half mocking.

"I want you to put it in a pail of water."

"Didn't they teach you anything about infernal machines in the KGB, Nick?" she said. "Water is the thing that sets some of these babies off."

He picked it up, gingerly.

"Now look what you're doing," she said.

"The mailman carried it," he pointed out. He put his ear to the package.

"Well?"

"Nothing," he said. "No ticking, anyway."

"So what do you want to do with it?"

"I'm thinking."

She went over to the phone. "I'm calling the cops."

"No," he said. "I don't want that. Then you'll really see the headlines."

"Well," she said, suddenly positive, "I don't think it's a bomb, anyway."

"How do you know?"

"I have a feeling, Nick," she said.

"That's very unscientific," he said. He picked it up.

"Watch yourself," she cautioned.

"I'm going to take it into the garden, dig a deep hole, and bury it," he announced. "Too bad if it's a box of cigars."

"I'm not sure you—" she began, but he said:

"You go ahead and make breakfast. I won't be long."

"I think you're crazy," she said.

"Well, you're the one who says it isn't a bomb. I'm just playing safe."

Suddenly she was alarmed.

"No, leave it. I *am* calling the police. . . ."

But he had already disappeared. She heard him close the back door.

She stood undecided, and suddenly she was terribly afraid. "Nick," she screamed, and then the explosion rocked the cottage.

"Nick," she cried again and headed for the garden.

He came toward her through the kitchen. He looked a little shaken.

She threw herself into his arms, and they held each other tight.

"Are you all right," she sobbed.

"I'm fine, babushka," he said with a half-smile. "But it blew out the bathroom window, I'm afraid."

"What happened?" she gasped.

"I put the package on the lawn and went to get a spade. That's when it went off."

"You sure you aren't hurt?"

"It takes more than that," he said. "It wasn't much of an explosion really, only a couple of ounces of explosive, I think. Of course, if we had been on top of it . . ."

"Oh God."

There was a hammering on the door.

"Are you okay in there?" came a muffled voice.

"That's Mr. Hopkins, from next door," said Gail. "He must think there's been an earthquake."

"Get rid of him. Tell him anything. Just get rid of him," ordered Nicolai.

Half an hour later she had stopped shaking.

"They wanted to kill you, Nick, do you realize that?" said Gail.

"Oh no. You're wrong. That little thing was only a calling card."

Washington

Bishop threw the FBI report across to Spence.

"You read this?"

Spence nodded.

"Well?"

"Pretty clumsy," said Spence. "You'd think if they're going to mail a bomb, it would be at least strong enough to wreck the place and kill everybody in it."

"You would think so," Bishop said thoughtfully.

"What's the term Galov used, 'a calling card'? Why bother?"

"War of nerves," said Bishop.

"Maybe they're thumbing their noses at us?"

"Maybe."

"Well, it proves one thing," said Spence. "They're out to get him. If he's right, this is just to put him on edge. Like hammering nails into the scaffold outside the death cell." He paused. "Carl, don't you think you should advise her to move the hell out of there?"

"Bob, she's not our responsibility," Bishop said harshly. "She's chosen her fucking bed. Let her lie in it."

New York

It was, for Moscow, a rather lengthy message to send to Valerian. It came via diplomatic radio channels through the Soviet UN mission in a code only decipherable by the KGB control in New York.

For Valerian, it was important personally as well as officially.

The instructions were peremptory, and had to be obeyed:

1. In view of the disappearance of your contact from circulation, it is wiser for you to leave your post, in case you have in any way been compromised. You are therefore being recalled, and will be reassigned to new duties on arrival in Moscow.
2. Your recall in no way reflects on your performance and is ordered purely as a security precaution.
3. You are booked to take the Saturday Aeroflot flight from Kennedy Airport straight to Moscow. Your official reason for your departure will be "family matters."
4. You will perform one last assignment before you depart. This is an important operation, and requires a short journey to Ossining, in New York State. Kravechenko will give you your special instructions personally.

Kravechenko was the chief of Valerian's detachment. He was better known as a member of the Soviet UN delegation specializing in economic problems of the Third World.

Almost ceremoniously, Valerian burnt the flimsy paper, and watched the ashes float down into the toilet bowl of his little apartment. Then he flushed the water. They had all been taught that even ashes could be traitors.

He had memorized his orders, as had become almost second nature to him. Kravechenko would give him his precise instructions tomorrow morning. He would carry them out later tomorrow, or on Friday. And then, on Saturday, home to Lydia and little Petrov and his darling little Maryka. He adored his family, and he made a mental note to buy Lydia something nice at Tiffany's, and some good toys for the kid at F.A.O. Schwarz. Having a diplomatic passport, he didn't have to worry about customs.

That was especially useful in view of the little armory he carried in a brown attaché case with combination locks.

Paragraph two of the signal from Moscow had pleased him exceedingly. The fact that Moscow went to the special trouble of reassuring him that his recall was in no way disciplinary showed that they were pleased with him. He felt that was only just. After all, he had done some nice, professional work in the United States.

He had really enjoyed it too, particularly the opportunities it had given him to see something of California and Arizona.

Valerian felt justified in having a little private celebration. He might as well make the most of it, since he wouldn't be in New York much longer.

He decided to treat himself to a magnificent dinner at Sardi's. And he would book a table at the Four Seasons for Friday night, the eve of departure. After that, he could face Moscow cuisine for quite a while.

Ossining

"Get away from that window," Nicolai said sharply.

Gail was sitting in the armchair, watching television. "Nick, I always sit here," she protested. "What's the matter."

"It's too near the window." He had been getting increasingly edgy all afternoon.

"You're terribly jumpy," said Gail.

"Well, it's too damn quiet," he muttered. "And never sit in a direct line with the window. It's asking for trouble."

Maybe this was the time to tell him. "I phoned Washington today," she said.

He stopped pacing. "What for?"

"I told Bishop you needed a vacation."

"The hell I do."

"I said you've been wearing away your nerves and needed a break."

"I bet he was very concerned."

"He was, as a matter of fact. He said why don't you and I take a trip to Florida. Have some sunshine."

"He said *that?*"

"At government expense, no less."

Nicolai frowned. "Why?"

"What do you mean, why," Gail said indignantly. "He understands people. He knows the strain you've been under. He cares."

"I bet."

"Well, you *are* his responsibility. At least, the government's responsibility."

Nicolai looked at his watch.

"That's the third time you've done that," Gail complained. "Are we catching a train?"

He laughed for the first time that day. "You're right, Gail," he said sheepishly. "I'm getting a bit jittery, with us stuck in this—this prison town. Ossining! Why did they ever bother to build that penitentiary. Why didn't they just dump the gangsters in this place, and leave them to rot?" He rubbed his hands. "Florida will do us a world of good. I can make love to you all day in the sun. When are we off?"

"Bishop will let us know."

He swung on her. "There. You see what I mean? He was just using the right words. You don't let the animals out of their cages."

"Don't be ridiculous. It has to be arranged. They've got to fix accommodations. Set up security. It'll be quite soon, I promise you."

He said nothing.

"Nick?"

"Yes?"

"You would like to go, wouldn't you?"

"Of course," he said. "Of course I want to get out of this place."

"You sure you want me along?" Her voice was very low.

He came over and kissed her. "My darling," he said, "you're the reason I can face all this. Without you—what would I have?"

She reached up and pulled him down.

"Tell me again," she said.

Ossining

Valerian lay flat on the roof of the half-built garage across from the cottage, and once again looked into the living room through the telescopic lens of his sniper's gun.

It wasn't really his style. He liked the more sophisticated means of assassination. The gadgets. The little pellets jabbed into the body, the gas vials fired into the face, the hair-thin needles pushed into the spine. Lurking in the dark with a rifle was old-fashioned. But he had to obey orders. Kravechenko had given him special instructions, and this was the only way to carry them out.

Finding this spot was a real stroke of luck. It gave him a marvelous vantage. He had been watching Galov and the woman with some interest. Galov was very careful. He had made her move so that eventually his view of her was obscured. And Galov himself seemed to take great care not to stand in front of the window even fleetingly.

Valerian looked at his watch. At 1800 hours sharp he would fire. Then, across the roof, down some scaffolding at the back, into the hired car, and off to Manhattan. In a couple of hours, he would be enjoying dinner.

He wondered what was so important about Galov. He had never known Kravechenko to give such a detailed briefing. And to ask for it to be repeated word by word. Kravechenko knew his ability. He had never botched a job. In fact, they had usually left the actual venue and style of disposing of the target to him. The stamp dealer, the man in Beverly Hills, the job in Chandler, the painter in Central Park, he had chosen method and time. And hadn't it always worked perfectly?

But Galov they wanted handled in their own curious way.

Well, here goes. He focused on the window. His finger tightened on the trigger.

"Now," said Bishop. There was a shot from the roof next door to the garage, and Valerian reared like a stricken animal. His steel-rimmed glasses went awry. Desperately he tried to raise himself.

"Again," ordered Bishop into his walkie-talkie. The

marksman, concealed on the roof of the movie theater overlooking the garage, fired again.

The bullet ploughed into Valerian's skull, and not even a photo-fit picture could help anyone recognize his face anymore.

"Guess we all make mistakes," said Bishop.

"What's that?" asked Spence, appearing at his side out of the shadows. It had been a long stakeout, and he was cramped.

"Never mind," said Bishop, talking more to himself than to Spence.

New York

She had never seen him so cheerful, thought Gail, as she drove to New York with Nicolai.

Since the evening of the shooting he had become less jumpy, less worried. "I feel good," he said. "It's like coming out of the darkness."

"Don't be too careless," she cautioned.

For a moment, his face darkened. "What do you mean, careless?"

"They might try again. You have to be on your guard every minute."

"Oh," he said airily, "I'm not worried about *them*. I can live with that. No, it's convincing Bishop that mattered."

"Convincing him about what?"

"That I'm genuine. That I'm not playing a double game. He was waiting for proof. He's had his proof now. Even he can't deny they wouldn't try to kill their own double agent."

"I don't suppose they would," said Gail, slowly.

"They've done me a good turn," he went on happily. "If they hadn't made their attempts, I'd still be a question mark here."

"Have you thought what you want to do now?"

"Yes," said Nicolai. "I want to be useful to this country. Maybe I shall write a book, maybe I can be an interpreter."

In Manhattan, he looked up at the skyscrapers on Sixth Avenue.

"It *is* impressive, this heart of capitalism," he commented.

"We call it the Big Apple. You make it sound like a Marxist tract."

He laughed. "You must forgive my old conditioning emerging. It is still too recent. I will learn."

They had lunch at a French restaurant on West Fifty-sixth Street, and over coffee he suddenly asked: "Why do you stare at me like that, babushka?"

"I see a different man," she said.

He was slightly wary. "How can I be different? I am the same flesh, the same blood I always was. What is suddenly different about me?"

"I don't know," she admitted. "Maybe you're no longer afraid."

"Gail, I've done what everybody's been telling me to do. I've adjusted." He took her hand. "I think we should have that vacation, you and I."

"That would be nice," she said, but it sounded a little flat.

"I think you need it as much as I do, that break."

"It's funny," said Gail, "everybody is always telling me I should take a holiday. Could make a girl wonder why they're all trying to get rid of her."

"I don't want to get rid of you, my love."

She looked into his eyes. "But one day, perhaps?"

"What nonsense you talk, of course not." He looked at his watch. "Come on, let's go to the Metropolitan Museum of Art. All my life I've wanted to see it."

"Now?"

"Why not? It is my first day in New York. You have shown me Times Square and Broadway and Fifth Avenue. Now comes culture."

"Nick," she said, "I've got an idea. *You* go. I need to do some shopping. We'll meet in a couple of hours, how is that?"

He looked disappointed. "No. I will come shopping with you."

"What size bra do you wear?" she asked. "No, really, I need some makeup and some underwear. You'd be bored stiff. I'll send you to the museum in a cab, and then go on to Saks. We'll meet at five. At the Plaza, all right?"

"But tonight, we paint the town red," he insisted. He laughed. "I like that expression, painting it red. Maybe I should now say blue?"

She put him in a cab and then got into one herself.

Manhattan

But she did not go to Saks, and she did not do any shopping.

She got out on Riverside Drive, and on the fourth floor of a building with closed-circuit television she faced Bishop.

"Gail," he said, "I'm sorry it's been such a long time."

She nodded, tense.

"Sit down," he invited.

"Carl . . ." she began, and stopped.

"Why did you want to see me?" he asked.

The strain showed in her eyes. "It's Nick," she said.

"What about him?"

She braced herself. "I think you're right." It was a great effort. "He . . ."

"He is a double agent," he prompted her. "That's what you're trying to say."

She nodded.

"How did you find out?"

She got out her handkerchief, and blew her nose. "Lots of things," she said at last.

"Like what?"

"The package. The bomb." She was speaking rapidly now. "I had a look at the postmark on the wrapper. It was mailed the day before."

"Yes?" said Bishop.

"It was mailed the day *before* the newspaper story revealed his cover name and his presence in Ossining. Nobody local knew then."

"He mailed it himself," said Bishop, matter-of-factly. "It was a primitive little job. He didn't have access to any explosives. So he bought some weed killer, and sugar. Very elementary."

"You knew?"

"I want your reasons," said Bishop. "Why you now know . . ."

"My gun," she said. "He took the bullets out. When I looked at it this week, the magazine was empty."

"Did you tell him?"

"No. No. But he was the only one who could have done it. Why didn't he want me to have a loaded gun? Especially when we were supposed to be in such danger? Was he afraid I might kill one of his own people?"

"I think you need a drink," said Bishop.

"No." She was holding herself in check with an effort. "Just listen. I suspect the bomb and the sniper were set up after he realized that this was the test. That you were waiting to see if anybody would make an attempt on his life."

"That means he's already in touch with somebody?"

She nodded. "I was out shopping. Quite by accident I saw him in a phone booth, making a call. When I asked him about it, he was shaken. He said I'd made a mistake. But it was him, I swear. And why didn't he use the telephone in the cottage?"

"Because we monitor it."

"And who would he call, anyway? Who does he know in this country?"

"You see, Carl, I don't think he was ever meant to be killed. But he knew when they were going to try. That night, when you got the sniper, he was very much on edge. He knew the sniper would deliberately miss him. He didn't want me to sit near the window, just in case the bullet that was supposed to go wide hit me accidentally. . . ."

Bishop walked across to her and very gently put his hand on her shoulder.

"But he cares about you?"

She found it difficult to reply. She was choked up. But at last she said: "I think so. I just don't know anymore. I believed in him . . . I don't know. . . ."

"You know," said Bishop gently, "I did you a great injustice. I thought your emotions ruled your head."

She had a wan, almost pitiful smile.

"What happens to Nick now?" she asked in a low voice.

"Nothing at all," said Bishop, and he went back behind his desk. "Status quo. And you will go on living with him."

She stared at him, aghast. "I'm not sure I can. Not now. Not after this."

"I'm afraid you have to," said Bishop. "If he is what we all think he is, you'll be doing the greatest service you can. You'll be the double agent inside the double agent. It's a lot to ask, I know, Gail, but do you realize how important this will become? When he starts operating?"

She sat silent. She tried to say something, and then shut her mouth. Finally she came out with it: "Supposing we are all wrong. Supposing we're making a terrible mistake. Supposing he is everything he says he is and he only wants to get away from this dirty business, and it's we who are the traitors. It's we who are betraying him. Because we are so corrupted by this work that everything we see is suspicious, everything we hear seems a lie. Suppose we are committing the most awful injustice . . ."

Bishop sighed. "Everything is possible in this nasty little world, Gail. But I'll take odds on this one. I think we got his measure."

"But *suppose* . . ." she pleaded almost desperately.

"Then we'll all have to live with it."

She stood up slowly. "And you want me to go on? Just as I have? Pretending? Living a lie?"

"You must."

"And if I can't take it?"

"I have a shrewd feeling, Gail, that you're tougher than you give yourself credit."

"Maybe I don't want to be."

"Think of the man you love," said Bishop quietly.

"But I am," she cried.

"Not him," he said. "The one who died."

She stood rigid. Then, like somebody called to order, she turned around and walked to the door.

But before she opened it, she said to him: "I'll be in touch."

"I know you will, Gail," he said.

Manhattan

Nicolai's face lit up as she came toward him in the lobby of the Plaza. She was carrying a couple of little packages.

"I spent too much money," she said. "How about you?"

"It was beautiful. I must go back. What a wonderful place." He looked more closely at her. "You've been rushing about too much, babushka. You look a little tired."

She gave his arm a squeeze.

"I feel much better, Nick," she said, "now that I'm back with you."

ABOUT THE AUTHOR

George Markstein began his wide-ranging writing career as a Fleet Street crime reporter. He has been story consultant and feature writer in British television; his screenplay for the feature film *Robbery* won the British Writers Guild award. Two of George Markstein's credits in particular have made his name a familiar one in the U.S.: he wrote the screenplay for *The Odessa File* and created the popular TV series *The Prisoner*. His novels include *The Cooler, Chance Awakening,* and *The Goering Testament.*